Pastor Dan

God's gifts guide us down our trail. Thank you for sharing in part of my journey.

Warmest Regards.

Clay Burnham

Valley of Hate

Carrot Bedders had been a free spirit all his life, but when he finds a golden Wyoming valley he decides to settle down and raise cattle. With him is his childhood friend Abel Meagan and together they start building the life of which they had always dreamed. Then they meet the spirited Emily Patterson, who captures both of their hearts and drives a rift between them.

Now Meagan's dreams are of an empire and he determines to conquer a land no matter who stands in his way. Neighbouring ranchers are not slow to accuse Bedders and Meagan of rustling cattle and there is a crescendo of resentment and rage in the whole valley. Despite all this, Meagan's herd continues to grow and violence seems destined to erupt.

Soon Bedders must take a stand against his lifelong friend and somehow find a way to stop the hate before it consumes the valley and lead begins to fly.

Valley of Hate

Clay Burnham

A Black Horse Western

ROBERT HALE · LONDON

© Clay Burnham 2004
First published in Great Britain 2004

ISBN 0 7090 7434 4

Robert Hale Limited
Clerkenwell House
Clerkenwell Green
London EC1R 0HT

Typeset by
Derek Doyle & Associates, Liverpool.
Printed and bound in Great Britain by
Antony Rowe Limited, Wiltshire

CHAPTER ONE

They crested the grassy hill together, stirrups nearly touching, each man rising up a little in his saddle, their faces marked by youthful expectation and sudden hunger. Behind them was a herd of three hundred or so trail-weary cows; ahead lay their future.

They were a pair, these two, young and rangy and flushed with energy and desire. Each had a little bit of baby fat still on his early-twenties face, Abel Meagan more so than Carrot Bedders. The clothes they wore were like costumes: woollen pants, long-sleeved white cotton shirts without collars that had long since gone grey, high-heeled boots with small rowelled diggers, and sweat- and dirt-stained hats – Meagan a buff coloured fedora and Bedders a battered old Montana peak that may have at one time been the colour of snow.

Atop that nameless hill, the Wind River Range a snow-dappled, purplish haze off in the distance, standing beneath a buttery sun, the two men paused, their eyes locked on the valley below. It was a green land, several miles wide and more than twice that deep. The end of the valley disappeared in a wide sweep around an outcropping of rock the colour of a ripe apple. Close to that outcropping was a pond. An active stream fed the pond so that it was really not much more than a wide spot in the stream, but the water looked clean and clear and a dozen cattle cropped grass near it. There were trees on both sides of the water, too, cottonwood and bur oak and golden willow.

'Damn, if you wasn't right,' said Abel Meagan, his chocolate-brown eyes aglow. He had nearly come out of his saddle, leaning far over the neck of his weather-beaten roan mare, as if his whole body yearned for what lay below.

Although trail-worn, Abel Meagan retained some of his town-fed fullness and the hint of softness a young man gets when he hasn't worked sunup to sundown for weeks on end. Still, he was narrow of hip and muscular, with quick eyes and a jut to his jaw that gave him a chiselled appearance. He had soft brown hair that had paled under the constant sun along a month of trail driving, and it had grown full and a little wild.

Beside him, Carrot Bedders' smile was endless. A light shone in his eyes like a beacon down into that fertile valley. Although nearly empty of livestock, his mind's eye saw a large milling herd of white-faced cattle scattered about and a pineboard house not too large – at the edge of that cool pond, a corral filled with fine, fiery horses, and a hay barn bulging with golden bales. It was a strange sight for his mind to conjure. He had always been like a pebble rolling downhill. But this valley was magnetic and it called his name.

'A place for us to make a real start, friend,' Bedders said joyfully. 'Make our own way.'

'With land like this, Nix, we'll do more than that. We'll make our fortunes.'

Carrot Bedders wasn't listening. His mind was again swallowed by the dream. His narrow frame sat comfortably in the saddle for despite his youth he had spent nearly ten years in saddles such as this one, doing a man's job of work starting at the age of fourteen when he lit out for horizons that never ended. He was rangier than Meagan but broader across the chest and shoulders, a physique built on equal parts post-hole digging, calf wrestling, and hay bale lifting. He had done all of that work and more. He had ridden fence in the dead of winter, trail drove herds riding drag and swing and chewing in a day as much dust as he did beans, and he had fought a running gun battle with a rustling band of drovers gone bad. Much had he done in his short life, and all of it showed in the creased lines of his face, the rough and raw texture of his sun-browned skin, the lanky, rangy muscles of his lean frame. Only the mop of curly red hair, aglow with a golden halo in the bright early summer sun, and the easy, slightly mocking twist to the edge of his lips reminded of the youth he still was beneath the hard casing of a cowman. He was not even twenty-four years old.

'We got us a few more head down there,' said Meagan, with a nod toward the pond.

'There's a couple of big outfits to the east and west. The beeves probably belong to them.'

'They're strays,' Meagan told him. 'We'll give 'em our brand and that'll be that. Isn't like we didn't pick up a few strays on the way up here.' Meagan cast a sly grin at his partner.

It was big country and cows got lost every day. Bedders said nothing. For a moment they enjoyed the view in silence.

'You say that valley goes on?'

Bedders pointed toward the apple-red rock along the eastern slope of the valley. 'Goes around that outcropping for another couple of miles. Good grass all throughout the valley.'

'And water.'

'We'll do just fine down there. Plenty of room to grow. More than we'll need right now, of course, but that'll change in a couple of years.' Bedders' eyes filled again with the image of an expansive herd of bawling, white-faced cows. 'We'll build us a house over there maybe,' he added, climbing down from his piebald pony to point to a raised area toward the western edge of the valley.

Meagan stayed atop his roan, a veiled expression coming into his face. 'What is it, Abel?'

'Nix, you and I have been pals a lot of years. Even when you were gone, which was a lot of the time, we was still friends.'

'We drove that herd up here and managed to stay friends, too, didn't we?' Bedders laughed easily, remembering the difficult journey the two of them alone had just made. During the day was tough enough, but at night, riding circle around the herd, singing to them, sweet talking them through thunder and lightning and wolves and coyotes, they lost a lot of sleep, and perhaps a bit of their youth.

'We sure did.' Meagan looked away from Bedders and gazed back down on the valley with its long grass flowing in the light breeze and the cool pond rippling and glistening. 'But, Nix, I ain't never seen two friends fall out as quick as when they team up in business.'

'Well, that's others,' Bedders protested.

'Sure. And they all thought that, too, I expect.' Meagan looked down on Bedders now from atop his roan, his face compacted into a look of deep concern and sincerity. 'I don't want that happening to us, Nix. You've been a pal,

8

coming back for me like you did and cutting me in on this. Oh, I know I did my share helping to wrangle them beeves, and I took as many night turns as you did.'

'Sure, we're partners,' Bedders cut in.

'But now that we're here I think we oughta make a go of it each on our own.' Bedders kicked a stone and watched it roll downhill, gathering dust and pebbles along the way.

'It'll be a lot harder that way, friend.'

'Sure it will. Why, this just can't be easy any way you slice it. But if we make it, it'll be ours. All our own. Beholden to nobody.' Now Meagan climbed down from his horse and went to Bedders. 'You've got to understand, Nix, what I've done in my life. It ain't been nothing. Not a damned thing have I accomplished. I've been working for other men my whole waking life.'

Bedders smiled and laid a hand on Meagan's shoulder. He could see a strange desperateness come into his friend's face, a little bit of a wild look in his eyes.

'Well, whata ya think I been doing? This is my chance, too, to work for myself.'

'Sure,' Meagan said, tearing away, 'you've worked for others. But you've done it out here, under these wide-open skies. You've ridden and roped and raised hell since you were fourteen. But me. I've clerked and swept barns and kept books for other men who didn't know the first thing about business. All of it from inside of four walls, and for what? Pennies. Pennies dropped at my feet like I was some street beggar. This is my chance, Nix, to do things my way, the way I've always believed they should be done.'

Bedders looked down into the valley, so serene and alive. 'You want to divide this valley?'

'It's yours, Nix. You found it. That's up to you. I just know that now that I'm here I've got to try and make it on my own.'

'This first winter will be hard. We won't have time to help each other build a house.'

'No. We'll build one together for now. A shack down by the pond, it won't be much. But it'll hold us through winter. We'll get our cows fat this summer and then come spring we'll combine our brands and drive them to market. After that we can turn our attention to making real homes for ourselves.'

Bedders climbed up on to his piebald and turned away from the view. 'Come on. We ain't doing nothing without getting them beeves into the valley.'

'Sure,' Meagan said, smiling, 'that's right, Nix. First things first.'

Milling at the bottom of the hill, the herd parted to accept the return of the men. They were restless creatures, smelling water nearby, and were easily turned toward the wide valley opening. It was a job slowing their pace as the smell of water grew stronger. Several of the strange cows looked up briefly then returned to cropping grass.

The cattle settled, Meagan loped out of the valley to where they had left a buckboard pulled by a team of two horses. He hawed at the animals to get them moving and drove the riderless rig into the valley. Aboard was their meagre outfit: tools, food, clothes, and the like. Meagan had taken his last wages from Parmenter's mercantile and bought the supplies. Bedders had furnished the buckboard and horses. That rainy afternoon, in the mud and on the last cold snap before spring thaw, Meagan had loaded the buckboard himself. In the three years he had worked for Parmenter this was the first wagonload of supplies he had ever put aboard with enthusiasm.

They set up camp, pitching a tent and gathering stones for a campfire. Meagan seemed content to sit in the shade of a cottonwood that whispered in the soft breeze and look out on the valley. It had been a long journey with just the two of them riding herd and he thought sitting on something quiet and still was a grand reward for their efforts.

Bedders, though, was anxious to ride. There was more to see beyond that red streaked outcropping of rock that hung from the hillside like a ripe apple on a tree. The valley went on, and Bedders wanted to as well.

Nervous energy driving him, Bedders stayed atop his piebald and joyfully choused the cows, getting them all to the pond to drink. He had just crossed the feeder stream when he noticed several riders approaching.

'Get up, Abel, we've got company,' he said. His pistol was still rolled up in the blanket tied behind his saddle so he pulled at the Remington in his saddle boot to make sure it would clear quickly if needed.

Meagan hopped to his feet and climbed aboard his roan, kicking the animal into a gallop. He rode out from camp a quarter of a mile then skidded to a stop, drawing the Colt's pistol from his hip. The riders – four of them – didn't rein up immediately, even though Meagan's gun was in plain view. They continued on until their horses were nosed up to the roan, then stopped.

Bedders cursed his partner for rashness and rode out after him, stopping a few dozen yards away and to the right of Meagan.

'Who are you?' asked one of the riders. He was tall and beefy with hands like bear claws and leathery skin browned by years in the sun. His horse seemed to sag underneath him.

All of the riders were scowling and fidgeting in their seats. No man's hand was far from his gun, whether he wore it in a holster about his hip or had a rifle sheathed in a saddle boot.

'We're drovers,' Meagan said, slowly.

'That I can see,' the man said sharply. 'What I want to know is what're you doing on Cavanaugh land?'

Bedders smiled. 'We're not on anyone's land, mister. And that's a fact. I checked in Lander before driving up with my herd.'

'Them cattle have the Cavanaugh brand,' the man said, tossing his head toward the valley. 'This is Star-M range.'

'Must not be too big an outfit,' Meagan said. He looked back at Bedders, a gleam shining in his eyes. Bedders squinted pointedly. It was a look of warning, but his friend ignored it, a mischievous grin growing across his face, and turned back to the riders. 'Why, there cain't be more'n thirty head of yo'rn loose on this whole range. You couldn't make enough selling them cows for beef to pay for their feed. Unless of course they's milk cows and you come for the afternoon milking.'

One of the men reached toward his gun but the fellow with the big hands stopped him. A dark red glow had come into his face. His black eyes were large and cavernous and they bore out at the young drover with a powerful hatred. He stepped down from the saddle, his horse grunting in relief, and crossed to Meagan.

'Step out of that saddle,' he commanded.

'Oh, dear, have I made a mistake?' Meagan asked, still grinning.

'You surely have. Now step down.'

Very deliberately and very loudly Bedders cocked his rifle. The riders, who had been intent on their man, anti-

12

cipating bloody vengeance for Meagan's insult, turned their eyes carefully to Bedders. The big man froze.

'We've had a long, hard drive, men,' Bedders said. The rifle he held crooked in his arm was loosely aimed in their direction. 'I'm sure you know what that's like. My friend and I are right friendly except when prodded or without sleep for days. We have no quarrel with you and mean no insult. But this is not Cavanaugh land. It's ours now. You're welcome to your cows, but we want you gone.'

Without turning the big man said, 'Are you planning on shooting me if I teach your friend a few manners?'

'You know, Nix,' Meagan said, 'I've been thinking on it. I think this big fella needs a lesson in manners hisself.'

The Cavanaugh rider let a slow grin stretch across his face. 'I know my boys will let this play out without guns, won't you boys?'

The other riders were grinning, too. Each nodded his head vigorously, laughing. 'Go ahead, Lincoln,' one of the other riders said, 'we'll see to that crippled ol' steed of yo'rn.'

'I think,' said Bedders with quiet forcefulness, 'you should apologize, Meagan, and let this go.'

Meagan chuckled. 'How ironic. After a month on the trail the wild range rover is the careful one, and the timid store clerk is ready to bust out fighting.'

With a sudden jerk, Meagan lashed out with his boot, catching Lincoln on the chin and sending the big man flopping to the ground. Meagan jumped out of the saddle landing atop Lincoln, awkwardly straddling the big man's chest. Going down to one knee, Meagan balled his fist and slammed it into Lincoln's face. A gout of blood shot out from the man's nose and he let out a rumbling roar.

Bedders looked over to the other three who were all sitting, their arms folded away from their guns. Each of them was still smiling, their faces eager with anticipation.

Meagan was laughing, too, as he drove another powerful blow down at Lincoln. But the blow never landed. Lincoln's hand shot out and enveloped Meagan's fist. Then, with a mighty tug, the big man jerked Meagan off his feet, tossing him to the ground. Meagan yelped in pain as his arm was twisted.

Slowly, Lincoln got to his feet. With the back of his hand he swiped blood away from his nose. Seeing his hand bloody brought a new fire to his eyes. He reached down and plucked Meagan off the ground, holding him up by the back of his shirt. With his bloody fist he backhanded Meagan, sending the rangy youth pinwheeling to the dust.

Bedders had been watching helplessly when a shot was fired. For a moment he almost fired his rifle at the three riders until he saw two more galloping up, guns in hand, and skidding to a stop.

'Lincoln!' one of the new riders yelled. He was an older man, although not much past his thirties. He had a full head of grey-blond hair and craggy lines filled his face. He was a big man, although not as big as Lincoln. Still, he rode tall and majestically, and his eyes had a depth of kindness Bedders found contrary to the cruel tone of his voice.

'What the hell are you doing? You want to kill that boy?'

Lincoln let go of Meagan, who collapsed to the ground in a heap.

'Yes, sir, Mr Cavanaugh. I believe I do.'

Cavanaugh shook his head angrily. Then he cast his gaze over to Bedders. 'What are you two doing here?'

'That's Abel Meagan and I'm. . . .'

'Didn't ask your damned names,' Cavanaugh interrupted roughly.

'. . . and I'm Carrot Bedders.'

'Carrot, huh?' Cavanaugh said. He glanced up at Bedders' red curls and a grin appeared briefly on his face. 'I guess that's right.' He took a deep breath and let it out slowly. 'I'm Amos Cavanaugh. I run the Star-M. One of my men came to get me when Lincoln spotted a strange herd and drovers on the range. Thought there might be trouble.'

Lincoln had stepped back to his horse and was wiping his bloody nose with a dusty kerchief. Meagan had managed to sit up. He nursed a sore arm and a bloody nose, and he seemed a little dazed as he wobbled slightly on his seat.

'I guess that's right,' said Bedders.

'Yeah. Well, I own this land, son. . . .'

'No, sir. You do not. I've been to Lander. This is open range. And we aim to homestead on it.'

Cavanaugh took another long, slow breath, his eyes never leaving Bedders. For his part, the youth returned the rancher's stare with calm sureness.

'We sometimes graze this land, though not much,' Cavanaugh admitted. 'It's a good place to find our strays.'

Bedders nodded. 'There were a few head scattered about when we arrived. If they're yours, you're welcome to them, of course.'

'Fact is we wouldn't've even been this far outside our range if we weren't looking for strays.'

Lincoln said, climbing into this saddle, 'I'll go round 'em up.'

'No,' Cavanaugh told him. Dull confusion passed over the big man's face. Cavanaugh continued with Bedders. 'You'll be spreading your herd out tomorrow. I'd be obliged if you'd bunch my cows up and chouse 'em to the mouth of the valley. I'll have a couple of my men pick them up tomorrow.'

Again Bedders nodded. 'OK.'

Glancing down at Meagan, Cavanaugh asked, 'Is he going to be all right?'

'Sure,' he told the rancher, a smile cracking his stoic features. 'He'll be right as rain tomorrow.'

Cavanaugh turned his horse and the others followed his lead. He was about to gallop off when he looked back at Bedders.

'You've seen the trail, of course, to get you down to the UP come this fall,' the rancher said. 'And you know where Lander is for supplies. There's a cut at the elbow of this valley that will take you right into town, just about. Saves a trip around the hills. And you can take a buckboard through.'

'Much obliged, Mr Cavanaugh. 'Though we won't be doing a fall round up this year. Need to breed the stock a bit first.'

'I guess that's right.'

Cavanaugh nodded once then nudged his mount into a gallop and led his men away.

Bedders dropped from the saddle, grabbed his canteen, and ran to Meagan. The store clerk had a dazed look in his eyes still but they were beginning to focus behind the welts and the bruises and the slow realization of pain. He looked up at his friend, a dopey, half-drunk look in his face, and Bedders laughed.

'Your eyes are bigger than your stomach, friend.'

Meagan took the canteen and swilled the warm liquid, splashing it around in his mouth, then spit out a pink-tinted mouthful. 'Don't I know it!'

Bedders got a fire going and brought supplies from the buckboard. He had seen game in the hills – deer, some elk, rabbit, and even what looked like a stray sheep. But he had no strength left with which to hunt. The long drive and the tense few minutes with Lincoln and Cavanaugh had left him drained. So he made coffee and pan biscuits and fried up some bacon. The buckboard held several cans of beans but Bedders had had his fill of them on the trail. They would go into the larder for the lean times he knew would be coming.

By the fire, with the last of the coffee, Meagan recalled with amusement the brief fight with Lincoln. This surprised Bedders, who had seen his friend turn mean and spiteful at times when others got the better of him. Just before they left Spearman for the last time Meagan had nearly beaten a man unconscious over some petty comment made about his wearing an apron in the mercantile. He had tried not to think about why Parmenter, the storeowner, had offered no hand or word of encouragement as Meagan packed to leave the next day. Meagan had been surly, embittered; Parmenter had simply been relieved.

'That man had the biggest hands what I've ever seen, Nix,' Meagan laughed now, slapping his knee, 'and that fist was like one of them bowling balls out of the Sears & Roebuck catalogue. Haw! He like to knock my head off.'

'You are lucky to be alive, pardner.'

Meagan's eyes turned cold with a sudden thought. 'Didn't see you jumping in.'

'I said my piece. You could have backed out of that with just a few words, if you had wanted to. But I had a gun on the others.'

'Aw, hell.' Meagan brightened again and laughed. 'I just had to try him! Imagine taking down a man-mountain like that? Why, we'd own this country!' Bedders laughed, tossing another stick on to the fire while Meagan swallowed from the canteen. But the taste left him grimacing.

'That water's right from the creek,' Bedders said. 'Tasted good to me.'

' 'Tain't this.' Meagan tossed the canteen aside. 'I'm the kind of dry water can't cure. Tell you what, tomorrow we'll get back up on our poor, tired old horses and ride on into Lander for a beer.'

'Not tomorrow.'

'We deserve it, pardner. Just the two of us hauling all these cattle up from Texas, dragging our own chuck wagon, and we didn't lose a head.'

A dark expression played on Bedders' face that the dancing shadows of the fire could not hide.

'Picked up a few is more like it.'

Meagan waved a hand. 'Hell, way I hear it you always pick up a few on the way. Strays, loners, whatever. At least most of them were unbranded.' The youth's smile encompassed his whole being – except his eyes. 'They're ours now. Ain't they?'

After a moment, Bedders agreed. 'They're ours.'

Morning found them both in their saddles. The sky was clear again and deep blue, but the sun would not clear the eastern rim of the valley until almost mid-morning. They let the cattle linger for a time at the pond, waiting for them to get hungry and mill around looking for soft grass. There was plenty of it in the valley.

With the cows on the move, Bedders and Meagan nudged the animals away from pond and spread them evenly about the valley floor. The herd wasn't big and the cattle, standing alone or in pairs, tended to fade into the backdrop. As they worked their own herd, they cut out the Star-M strays, and found a few animals from other outfits as well. These they bunched together toward the south entrance to the valley.

At midday, as they were ready to head back to their camp for dinner, Meagan whistled and waved, pointing toward the northwest elbow of the valley. A dust cloud rose up, disappearing against the rocky and tree-lined background. At the base of that cloud was a rider coming on fast.

Meagan stood up in his saddle and craned his neck as if that would give him a better view. He looked over to Bedders some hundred yards away and shrugged.

Something spat into the ground at the feet of Bedders' piebald, chipping rocks and dirt into a sudden spray. A crack echoed in the valley as the horse shied and whinnied.

Meagan looked over at Bedders, his face bunched with concern and confusion.

Another crack echoed just behind an angry buzzing that swept passed Bedders' ear. Bedders felt no confusion. That rider was shooting at them.

Sliding his Remington from its scabbard, Bedders brought the weapon to his shoulder and sited along the barrel toward the approaching rider. With deliberate motion he worked the lever and chambered a .44-40 round. Then, eye squinting, he squeezed the trigger.

CHAPTER TWO

Bedders' shot cracked loudly but the piebald stood its ground without fidgeting. In a panic, the approaching rider jerked at the reins of his horse sending the animal into an awkward stumble. The horse tripped and collapsed, then rolled and bounded up again, its eyes wild and red, leaving the rider down in the dust as it galloped off aimlessly.

The two young drovers put spur to horsehide and raced to meet the newcomer.

'Just hold it right there,' commanded Meagan. His Colt's pistol was drawn and cocked and pointed at the grey heap on the ground. Suddenly Meagan's eyes went wide and his mouth flopped open. 'You're a girl!'

Meagan's gun loosely rocked forward on his finger and nearly fell from his grasp before he collected himself enough to holster the weapon.

'Sorry, ma'am!' But he wasn't sorry. He wore a wide grin, as wide as his eyes that took in the curving shape of the young woman just now pushing herself up off the dust. Her rawhide skirt was long and frilled with small red tassels, but the hem of it had been lifted quite high in the fall. Pale, shapely legs were exposed to the sun.

Meagan jumped down and pushed out a hand to help her. Her eyes flashed like green lightning sparkling in the setting sun. Her high cheeks were flushed and her small, red-lipped mouth was twisted into a sneer. She slapped at Meagan's proffered hand as she darted about for her fallen rifle. When she found it the sneer on her face deepened into an animal-like snarl. Bedders' piebald had come to rest on the weapon, one ironshod hoof pressing heavily on the stock.

'You shot at a woman,' she said with barely controlled anger.

Bedders was not smiling. There was fire in his eyes, too, and a great deal of anger as he sat looking down at her. The young woman saw this but was not afraid. She stood and let her skirt fall to the tops of her hand-tooled brown boots. The skirt was twisted a little but she did not try to smooth it. She did not smooth or dust off the pretty white blouse and rawhide vest that clung to her obviously female shape. Nor did she try to straighten a mass of ash brown hair that had tumbled in a pile out of her black and white fringed sombrero when she fell.

She simply stood there, fists balled, anger rising from her sleek white throat and said, 'What kind of man shoots at a woman? And you'd kill a horse, too, wouldn't you?'

'If I had to.'

'Ma'am, I cannot apologize enough for our rough introduction.' Meagan had his hat off and held it close to his chest as he talked over the rim of it.

'Is that the way you always greet strangers?' Bedders asked. 'Shooting at them?'

'Those,' she said hotly, 'who are trying to rustle live-stock.'

'The truth is, ma'am,' Meagan said, shifting in front of

21

her gaze which had not lifted from Bedders, 'these critters is ours. We brung 'em up from Texas, all by our lonesome to start a ranch of our own.'

'You don't own this land.'

'No, but my friend there – he's Carrot Bedders and I'm. . . .'

'What kind of name is Carrot?' she asked, stepping around Meagan to glare at Bedders.

'Mine.'

Meagan was working to keep frustration out of his tone, but that only served to pitch his voice higher. 'And I'm Abel Meagan.'

'How do you do, Mr Meagan.' She turned to him, taking a deep breath, and held out a slim white hand. Meagan stood looking at it for a moment before grasping it firmly.

'Oh, very well, ma'am. Very well, indeed.'

Pivoting back to Bedders, she asked, 'And how do you know that this valley isn't owned, sir?'

'I checked.'

A sly grin came into her face and she said, 'I don't remember seeing you, or your friend, in town.'

'I went to the land office. Talked with a fella in a wheel-chair. An older man behind the counter. He showed me a map and various papers. He said we could homestead.'

'Now that you're here you'll have to go in and fill out some papers yourself, eventually. You can write, can't you?'

Bedders reddened and his lips compressed. 'Passably.'

'You're not very friendly, sir.' She was being playful now and that angered Bedders even more.

'You shot at me.'

'We forgive you that, ma'am. We surely do. It was an obvious mistake, what with us working the cows here. But

22

I can assure you we are rounding up Mr Cavanaugh's stock for him. Why, there's a bunch standing across the stream right now waiting for the Star-M boys to pick 'em up.'

'You've met Mr Cavanaugh?'

'Yes'm.'

She put a gentle hand to Meagan's face, turning it to shed some light on the swollen bruise of his right cheek and eye. 'Looks like you met Lincoln, too.'

'He sure did,' Bedders said with snort, forgetting his anger for a moment.

'Well!' The girl's face brightened with shining happiness and the force of it struck Bedders like a blow from the Star-M man-mountain. 'You can be friendly!'

'We can, ma'am. Both of us. Well, Carrot on occasion. But with me it's a right steady thing.'

The girl laughed, all of her adrenaline-charged anger and heat now dissipated. 'I can see that, Mr Meagan.'

'We needn't wait for the Star-M hands, ma'am. I can help you drag them beeves in if'n you like.'

'I'm no hand! And I'm no kin either. My name is Emily Patterson and I run the land office with that old man you met in the wheelchair. He's my father.'

'Miss Patterson,' Meagan said, taking Emily's hand solicitously, 'it will be my distinct pleasure to make his acquaintance when we get to town.'

Bedders snorted again. 'And here I thought you were the sheriff or some such, what with you taking on a gang of cattle thieves single handed.'

'This is good country, Mr Bedders. We haven't had a rustling problem in years and every one of us aims to keep it that way. Besides, Mr Cavanaugh is a family friend.'

Grinning, Bedders said, 'Now what kind of woman goes a-calling on a man?' He was feeling a bit peckish himself now, and was pleased to see he had prodded the girl a bit. She reddened again, from the neck up.

'I'm calling on business. Mr Cavanaugh has purchased some new land and I'm bringing the papers out to him.'

'More land. . . !' Meagan sputtered.

'Oh, don't worry. Not this valley. Something a little closer to his range.' Emily's horse had slowly wandered back toward her, tossing its head and snorting for attention. She went to it and caught up the reins, rubbing its neck and patting its flank. It seemed little worse for its tumble, but anxious to get moving.

Climbing into the saddle she said, 'I'll look forward to seeing you men in town. Perhaps we can leave this incident behind us.'

'Count on it, Miss Emily,' Meagan said. He motioned for Bedders to move then bent to pick up the rifle. The action and the barrel were fine, but the stock was imprinted with the piebald's hoofprint. Shrugging with apology, Meagan handed the weapon back to the girl.

Emily took the rifle, waiting a moment for Bedders to say something, but he remained silent. Yet he watched her ride off, following her movement intently, hardly blinking until she was out of sight.

Suddenly Meagan's hands were on him, pulling him from the saddle, gripping his shoulders. There was a grin that stretched across the youth's face and his eyes were wide and a little foggy.

'You got a concussion there, pardner?' Bedders asked, a grin spreading across his face, too.

'That is a fiery woman, Nix. A spitfire!'

'She sure is.' To his own ears the sound of his voice was a little more wistful than he intended. Hearing it, a cold light sharpened Meagan's sight.

'Now, you know I saw her first,' he said, his voice tinged with warning.

Bedders laughed. 'Friend, if you can manage that she-cat she's all yours!'

They ate their dinner on the run, Meagan too restless to sit down. In no time he was back up in the saddle chousing cows with frenetic energy. Bedders was afraid his partner would stampede the lot of them as he whooped and hollered, bouncing in the saddle like a jack-in-the-box. Eventually Bedders convinced the excited youth to join him in exploring the rest of the valley and they rode off at a gallop around the apple rock bend. Beyond was more greenery, the soft grass undulating in a whisper of a breeze. The valley stretched for several miles but was a bit narrower than the front end of the valley. The walls were higher here, too, steeper and more rocky. Mounds of talus formed rocky foothills on the northern slope. The southern slope was greener than the opposite rise and filled with better timber. The stream that fed the pond and then trickled away meandered through this section then cut into a small hole in the valley's sheer, rocky dead-end and disappeared. The hole looked like it might be big enough for a man to slip into if he was willing to get wet in the cold water.

The ride had done Meagan a world of good. His mind settled, his eyes not so wild, he began rounding up the rest of the Star-M cows and other strays that wandered about. By late afternoon they had formed another bunch of perhaps twenty cows and were ready to drive them back around the apple rock bend. Meagan was off toward the far end of the valley working a newborn calf toward a pile of rocks close to the northern slope.

'Giving you trouble?' Bedders said as he rode up.

'No trouble,' Meagan grunted. He was working his roan hard, keeping its front legs dancing trying to manoeuvre the frightened calf.

Bedders laughed. 'You know, if you just let the thing go it'll run back to its mama.'

'Why would I want that?' Bedders did not answer. He stared at his friend with cool eyes. 'Hell, Nix, she ain't got a brand on her.'

'Cavanaugh isn't stupid. He'll know his animal calved. And he'll know we held out on him.'

'He ain't gonna worry about one calf.'

'He will, Abel. He's the kind of man who'll do just that. And so will Lincoln.'

Speaking that name had been like a slap across Meagan's face. He reached up and touched his cheek and the welt that would smart for many days to come. Meagan's face went cold and dark.

'I figure I'm owed a calf or two for this.'

Bedders took a long, slow breath and tried a different tack. 'We've got to get along here, Abel. We're the new fellas and we've got to be good neighbours. I aim to be just that.'

'OK, Nix,' Meagan said, nodding. 'Hell, she's a scrawny one anyway.'

He let the calf free and it ran toward the bunch of cows at the bend. A short time later the two men had driven the strays across the stream, picked up the other bunch of strays, and then driven the small herd to the mouth of the valley. Still trail-trained, some of their own stock mingled with the strays and Meagan had to cut them out while Bedders drove the others further away. It was an exasperating game the animals played and it kept the two men busy for an hour until the Star-M riders arrived.

There were two of them, neither of which had come to the valley the day before. That was probably Cavanaugh's doing, Bedders thought. He didn't want any ill feeling from the previous day's encounter to spark a new incident. Bedders found he was beginning to like this man.

'Mr Cavanaugh says you got some of our strays,' a red-faced cowboy said. He wore a grin that Bedders imagined was a permanent fixture beneath bright blue eyes and coal-black hair.

'We've got more than that,' Bedders said. 'There's a few other strays mixed in, other brands we don't recognize.'

The black-haired man nodded. 'Sure. That'd figure. We can cut those out and deliver 'em to the right ranges.'

'Much obliged.'

The two Cavanaugh men circled around the cows and started hawing them forward. 'This all of them, then?'

'All we found.'

Meagan rode up then, chousing that stray calf in front of him. 'Don't forget this one, Nix,' he said with a grin. 'Wouldn't want to cheat these fellas out'n all they're due.'

The black-haired rider followed the calf into the herd. The animal ran right for a cow heavy with milk and began nuzzling at its belly. Riding a way he cast a meaningful glance back at Bedders, his eyes slitted and the permanent smile on his face a little sharper. The man thought that Bedders had tried to hold out on him. It was foolish thinking; holding out one calf could only invite trouble. But in that instant Bedders had been branded. The Cavanaugh men would think him a cattle thief, and a damn poor one at that.

Bedders looked over at his friend who was tossing a cheerful wave at the backs of the Cavanaugh men and wondered just how foolish Meagan had been.

It was the same childhood game Meagan had always played. Oh, Bedders had gotten into enough trouble on his own. He was a wild spirit, his mother had called him, and he had roamed far and wide even in those early days. Meagan had gone with him on occasion, but usually their play had been in town, pulling pigtails on girls they liked, letting lizards out in church, that sort of thing. Bedders had been caught often and the pastor had taken a switch to his backside, since his father had run off after a woman from a travelling medicine show. But every so often, when blame could not be placed squarely and convincingly on his growing shoulders, Meagan would speak up, his face angelic and his eyes guileless, and asked, 'Is this your frog, Nix?' Or something of the sort. Then all eyes would turn to Bedders and the pastor would again reach for the thin piece of hickory.

Bedders didn't mind, though. Meagan was a boon companion and even at that young age Bedders had had the wisdom to understand that boys were often cruel, even to those they loved.

But at age fourteen Bedders had had enough of town life. His mother had died and the pastor had taken him in. The man wasn't much of a father and his wife, so put upon by the man's domineering strictness, had no chance to be much of a mother to him. The hickory switch was so often slapped at his backside that he had thought it part of him, like some malevolent tail.

Without a word he had packed his few belongings, saddled his horse, a giant black that made him look small sitting atop it, and rode out of town. He had met Meagan on the road and told him goodbye. Anger and tears and hatred filled the youth and he lashed out. Bedders hadn't struck back. He got back aboard the black, riding away without a backward glance.

They had parted badly and the hole it left in him was huge. Eventually he got up the courage to write a letter to his friend and was thrilled when he received a reply. Within the cheerful words of that first letter was his friend of old and Bedders knew then that one day he would go back for Meagan.

After the Star-M riders left the valley, the two returned to camp. Bedders stoked the campfire, putting coffee and bacon and biscuits on to cook. Meagan took care of the horses, turning them into a rope corral. They spent a quiet evening and went to bed early, each surprised at how tired they were.

There was an awkward silence the following morning. With the stock spread out and grazing on their own, and with only the mouth of the valley to watch for straying cattle, they knew their next task was to build a shanty to live in. By midday, the tension was too great for Bedders to take.

'Look here,' he said to a lounging Meagan, who had thought to try fishing in the small pond, 'did you mean what you said yesterday about this valley?'

'I did,' said Meagan, soberly. 'It's your valley. You found it, so you decide what you do with it.'

Bedders pulled off his soiled hat and slapped it hard against his leg sending a small cloud of dust into the air. 'Well, hell, I thought I done that when I asked you to partner up with me.'

Meagan smiled deep and friendly. 'I can't help how I feel, Nix. I got to try it on my own. The valley's yours. I'll ride into Lander and check with that land agent to see what else is available.'

'You just want a chance to see that spitfire woman.'

'I shore do!' he said, his smile changing to a goofy grin.

'Aw, hell, Abel. I wanted us to go in on this together. To

share the valley. I didn't want you roaming off on your own.'

'It's gotta be that way, Nix. Now that I'm free of that helltown I gotta do this my way.'

'It wasn't no helltown, Abel,' he said, a flush of youthful memories washing over him.

'Not for you. You left.'

They fiddlefooted for a while, Bedders riding around, Meagan fishing. Toward suppertime they came together again.

'We could divide the valley,' Bedders said. He let loose with a gust of breath that had in it equal measures of exasperation and disappointment.

'Sure. It's big enough. We can make the pond and the stream the dividing line, right on through to the Apple Rock. There's about the same on each side of it.'

Bedders agreed. 'Which side you want? Now don't argue. You pick it.'

'OK.' said Meagan, looking around appraising the valley. 'I feel right comfortable on this side, Nix. Toward the mouth of the valley.'

'All right, it's yours. But how will I get my half of the herd out of here come roundup?'

'Well, hell, Nix, we're still friends. You just drive 'em on through! And I reckon you won't have any ill feeling if I cut through your side to get to Lander.'

'No. That'll be fine.'

'Might do it often,' he teased.

'I expect you might.'

Meagan was all smiles and energy. He put aside his makeshift fishing pole and stood with his arms spread wide as if trying to hold the entire range in his grasp. His eyes were big and round and, like Bedders had the day before, he was seeing a range filled with cattle. Cattle with his brand burned deep into their hides.

They divided up the white-faced stock the following morning. Bedders had thought they only had three hundred head, but it was more. A lot more. Well over four hundred. On the drive up he had looked the other way when Meagan had cast a wide loop over the lonesome strays and unattended bunches they had found. He figured it would even out, that they would lose as many as they took on. That was the way of the trail drive. There was always give and take and nobody thought ill of a cowman who turned up with a few head that bore another's brand. Everyone knew that the cowman had left some of his own behind.

A herd was a strange, living thing. Made up of hundreds or even thousands of cows it was bigger than its individual parts. It moved differently than a single cow would move. It was like an ocean with waves tossing and splashing in all directions. Losing a hundred head of your own wasn't unheard of, on the big drives, and Bedders had been on a few of those. They'd always ended the drive with near as many as they had started.

This was different. In his eagerness to build up the herd fast Meagan had become a cattle thief. Yet seeing his friend enjoy the freedom of his own land, working with him, side-by-side to cut down ash and pine from the hillside to build their winter shanty, talking with him through the endless nights of summer as their divided herd grew fat and lazy, he believed Meagan had acted unknowingly. Abel Meagan was no thief, Bedders told himself. He was a good man who had worked his whole life – since the age of ten – at jobs Bedders never could stand.

He remembered a time they had both taken jobs at the Johansson stables, sweeping out dung and forking hay to horses. It was painful work for a boy who only wanted to saddle a brilliant white mare from one of the stalls and ride her all day long. Temptation finally besting him, Bedders had done just that – and had been caught minutes later. But it had been fun and exciting, thrilling to a boy whose strict guardian kept him on a short leash. It was Meagan who stayed and finished the work meant for two boys, while Bedders was having his fun and later was getting his hide tanned.

Meagan would settle into the monotonous, sometimes frightful existence of a cowman, of that Bedders was certain. With each passing day the memory of their drive north would dull a little more and the numbness of riding herd on a bunch of motionless cattle would set in. His enthusiasm would wane, although he would plod onward as he always had.

The strange thing to Bedders was that he did not see that same fate for himself. He had driven cattle before, and worked other men's ranches and he knew about the numbness of the job. But looking out across the valley he felt a pang of pride deep in his chest, a feeling he had never before experienced. He was building something; something that would be strong and good, and something that he would pass along to his son, a legacy never bequeathed to him. That notion led his thoughts to Emily Patterson and her vibrant features blossomed in his mind. They came unbidden like the scent of honeysuckle on the wind, cheering his lonesome heart and filling him with a lightness of spirit. Then he felt another pang, a deeper one like a wound torn into his chest. He looked out across the range to the small pond where Meagan sat fishing for something that wasn't there and he knew the pain he felt now was nothing compared to what would come.

CHAPTER THREE

Bedders had made a pit out of the talus on the northern slope of his range, piling stones by hand in the mud and arranging them in a wide circle. It was back-breaking work, depressing standing for hours in the cold spring rain. His clothes were soaked through and he felt a chill deep in his bones.

To the pit he dragged dead cattle. One at a time he roped the lifeless hunks of flesh by their back legs and dragged them. Wherever they had fallen, by the pond or back into the deepest corners of the canyon, he would rope and drag them. One mile, two, three. It didn't matter. There were too many of them to deal with where they lay.

So he built the pit and dragged the carcasses to it. He skinned those that had salvageable hides then tossed the maggot-infested flesh into the pit. At first the piebald shied from the dead animals, the smell of them deep in its nostrils. It jerked and fought to run away but Bedders had trained the horse too well. After a time the animal became inured to the smell and the sight of death, hanging its heavy head, plodding through the mud. The smell of death was in Bedders, too, so deep that he thought he would never be washed clean of it.

When he had gotten all the dead cattle into the pit, and the rain had stopped, he poured the last of his kerosene over the carcasses and lit them ablaze. The fire burned for days.

During the happier days of summer, he had explored his end of the valley and found a series of small caves that dented the rocky hillside. He had explored each and found none of them went back very far. But they were dry and comfortable inside so he had laid in a supply of firewood to keep it dry. To the caves now he took the hides and laid them out to cure. Most of them would be ruined; he didn't have the proper tools to dry the leather. But he would be able to make some ropes and replacement latigos for his saddle and have enough left over to sell in town.

He needed to do that now, sell what he could. The winter had been near ruinous. Fifty head were gone, killed by cold and lack of grass. Bedders' side of the valley, around the dogleg of Apple Rock, was smaller and had been less densely packed with grass than Meagan's side. It was lower, too, which he hadn't known at first, so water tended to collect in spots. After grazing the entire summer, there wasn't much grass left for the winter.

Bedders realized he had made a grave mistake. He should have bunched his small herd and worked them in sections across the valley, moving them just before they ate a section bare. That would have given each area time to grow new grass and would have left something for winter. Now he wasn't sure how the grass would come back, or if it would. Much of the valley was a quagmire.

He and Meagan did not talk much that winter, at least about their herds. Bedders could tell though, from the tenseness in Meagan's face, that his friend was not faring much better. Meagan was no hand. He'd never worked cattle. Several times Bedders tried to broach the subject of joining forces again, but Meagan laughed it off saying he'd be as big as Cavanaugh one day, the way he was going.

Meagan spent a lot of time outside their shanty. It wasn't much warmer inside than out so being atop a horse and riding was the best way to keep from freezing. He'd be gone for days sometimes, then come in shivering and near feverish. Bedders figured Meagan was taking long rides into town to see Emily Patterson, at least some of the time. For the rest of it he couldn't say.

Snow fell in earnest in early November and stayed in the valley until March. But it wasn't very deep and most of the cattle could scratch through it for what little grass they could find. Bedders spent much of his time in the caves, which were warmer than the shanty. He found a small rise not far from the pass that led to town and began imagining a house built on it. At first it wouldn't be much bigger than the shanty, but it would be better built than that hastily constructed shack. Sitting on the rise would give it a good view of the valley and keep it from the winter-wet lowlands.

As the weather warmed, and after burning the cattle carcasses, Bedders rode back to the shanty to look for Meagan. His friend was gone, though the herd was still there. But something was wrong. He began riding through the herd, looking at the strange black-faced and familiar white-faced cows, counting them. There were more than four hundred head scattered about the range when there should have been less than two hundred.

Bedders dismounted by one of the black-faced cows and had just begun searching for the animal's brand when a shot rang out. He turned to see two riders galloping toward him.

'Hold up there, you!'

The speaker wore a heavy, matted beard, a tall hat, and was as muddy as his grey horse. The other was clean-shaven, shorter than the first, a little plumper, and he wore a fairly new leather hat. Each had a pistol out and aimed toward Bedders.

'What're you doing with them beeves?'

'I think these are strays,' Bedders said, keeping the cow between him and the others.

'They're nothing of the sort. This is Meagan land and these are Meagan cows.'

Something heavy sank deep into Bedders' gut. He looked across the range and saw more than twice the amount of stock Meagan should have. He didn't have to do much wondering to imagine where they had come from. There were several horses, too, standing quietly inside a rope corral.

'Are you Bedders?' the shorter man asked.

'That's right.'

'Well, that's OK, then,' he said to the other, motioning for them to holster their guns. But the bearded man did not move. His hard, black eyes did not lift from Bedders. 'M'name's Glen Lefferts,' the shorter man offered with a quick smile that didn't suggest friendliness, 'and this here's Lloyd Baxter. We're riding for Mr Meagan.'

The shock of that hit him hard but before he could question them Meagan rode up.

'There you are!' he said with a friendly wave and wide grin. 'Why, you look plum bewildered, friend.' Meagan got down off a black mare and came over to shake his friend's hand. 'I haven't seen you almost all winter. Fellas, this here

36

is just about the best friend a man can have, Carrot Bedders. I haven't seen him in a while, boys, so we're goin' inside to jaw for a while. You can start branding. I'll be along.'

The two men nodded then reined their horses over and trotted off.

'Looks like you had a good winter,' said Bedders, a hard edge in his voice.

'Let's go inside. I'm hungry.'

Meagan pushed into the shanty, the plank door unstable on worn wooden hinges. Meagan went to the rock stove they had built last summer and stoked the embers, adding a few small pieces of wood. Bedders hadn't been in the shanty for over a week, but apparently Meagan had used it recently. He took a coffeepot and filled it with water from a metal pail and with grounds from a sack of Arbuckle's. He set this on a rock near the growing flame before grabbing two old tin cups and setting them on the rough-hewn table. Tree stumps served as chairs.

'Nix, I know what you're thinking about them two hundred beeves, and you're just wrong about it. I spent the whole of winter out looking for strays. Why, I only roped those that didn't have a brand, or the brand was long grown over and unrecognizable. You just know folks gave up on those critters. I spent a lot of long, cold days out there, friend. But I knew I just had to have more stock to make a go of this ranching business.'

Meagan carved slices of bacon from a slab kept in a wooden box covered by a greasy towel. He tossed these into a frying pan and put that over the fire, too.

'Looks like your beeves came through the winter all right, though.'

'Well, I lost me some head, Nix. I sure did, and it

pained me, too.' Meagan turned the bacon. 'How many did you lose?'

'About fifty.'

'Damn! That's too bad.' He checked the pot to see that the coffee was beginning to boil. 'What are you going to do now?'

Bedders thought for a moment. 'We'll see what happens this spring and summer.'

'That's good thinking,' Meagan said, nodding. 'Give it some time. Why that herd of yor'n'll come back right as rain.'

'How about you? You'll be driving this fall?'

'I expect not. I'll have a good number of calves and I'll want them to fatten and grow some.'

'How're you going to pay those men out there?'

'Lloyd and Glen? Why, I saved up some from all those years of working. Clerking don't pay much but it adds up if you don't have anything to spend it on.'

Meagan's voice was no longer loose, and there was a hard look in his eyes. He kept his gaze away from Bedders, tending to the coffee and bacon.

'You've got them men out there branding a bit early, don't you?'

'Naw, ya see I'm going to take part of the herd out in a few weeks, as soon as the rain stops, and sell them for some quick cash. In my roaming this winter I heard tell of a fella whose got a herd of longhorns to sell cheap. I'll buy 'em and the boys and I'll run 'em back here to fatten them up. Next year we'll go to town, that's for sure.'

Meagan took the pot and poured coffee into their cups, then he set the frying pan down on the table between them. Licking his fingers, he picked up a piece of bacon and shoved into his mouth.

'We'll stick around for a few weeks yet. I've picked out a spot to build a house of my own.'

'You've got plans.' Bedders took a slow sip of his coffee.

'Yes, I do. I told you that the first day we came on to this valley.'

'I guess that's right.'

'Now you stick with this shanty for a while, Nix. When me and the boys come back we'll help you build a right nice place on your end of the valley. Picked a spot yet?'

'Yes.'

The tension in the room had been growing. Bedders felt anger rising in him and at first he didn't exactly know why. Meagan's cocky attitude had much to do with it. He was a greenhorn talking like an old time rancher. A big shot, looking down on Bedders. He knew the feeling was childish. His friend was doing well, and he should be happy for him. In less than a year Meagan appeared to have taken easily to a way of life Bedders had spent all his adult years living. It was jealousy, he recognized finally, and he hated himself for it. But there was something else niggling at the back of his mind, a growing concern for his friend. In less than a year Meagan had done too well, better than he should have. Bedders struggled with those emotions, too, as he sat talking to Meagan. Now he buried both of them, the jealousy and the concern, and decided to start worrying about himself.

'You'll be gone a while for them longhorns?' Bedders asked.

'About two months. I'd be much obliged if you'd keep an eye on my stock while I'm gone, Nix,' he said, his face cheerful again. 'That'll keep you close to the range. Because I wouldn't want you going to town too often, ya hear? I still got my eye on that Emily gal.'

Bedders pushed a slim smile across his face, lifting the coffee cup to his lips. 'I understand, Abel.'

Later, finishing his second cup of coffee, Bedders watched as Meagan and his crew built a rude house not much better than the shanty. Meagan had found a small rise that looked down on the valley and had a good view out beyond it, too. Some of that land outside the valley was open range and Meagan would need it to graze the new stock. But there wasn't much water out there. The grass didn't grow nearly as high there as it did within the valley. Meagan would need a lot more range if he brought in too many head. He'd be butting up against Cavanaugh land, then, to the northwest, and land belonging to a smaller rancher, 'Pistol' Nate Danelles, to the southeast. No matter how bloated Meagan got he just didn't believe he could take on those men and win.

After the new house was built Meagan and his men rode out of the valley, pushing a hundred cows ahead of them. The rains had stopped and the sun was beginning to add a steady glow to the range.

Bedders had been in a funk watching Meagan. Now that the other was gone he shook himself free of his gloom and decided to build his own house. With the old tools they had brought with them, Bedders went up into the hills and felled a dozen and more fair-sized pine trees and dragged them, using his two horses and even some cows, to the location he had found near the pass. He planed the wood and shaped and notched it and then left it to dry while he worked the piles of talus on the northern slope. Using cows again, and his horses, he dragged stones from the slope to the small plateau and began laying a foundation.

The days were endless, filled with tiresome work that left him exhausted but also cheered. He was building something. For too many years he had simply existed, taking what he needed and then moving on. Looking out on his dwindled herd he wondered if he was building something that would last. He wondered if the grass would come back as full as it had grown last summer, fearful that it wouldn't and he would lose more of the stock. He wanted to succeed. Not for the money or for the power of controlling a range, but for the simple pride of doing something well.

After the short foundation walls had been laid, Bedders searched for flat rocks that he would use for flooring. The animals dragged these up to the low rise and Bedders chipped at them and shaped them until they neatly fitted together. He built the doorway wide so he could eventually bring in a potbellied stove, and he even cut a window frame which he covered with a shutter on the outside and stretched leather on the inside. It would do until he could afford to buy oilpaper or perhaps glass.

He had twice gone into Lander for building supplies, and neither time had he seen Emily.

For a full day he struggled with pushing the centre roof joist up across the shallow roof. When it finally fell into place Bedders whooped so loudly that he nearly startled the cattle into stampeding. As it was his horses bolted and he had to spend an hour fetching them and calming them down. The rest of the roof went on quickly enough.

Throughout the spring, while building his small home, Bedders had put into practice his ideas for managing the land, and it paid off. He was able to keep the cows on one section at a time, which allowed the grass to re-grow and the seed to spread and grow new grass.

Meagan had been gone nearly a month when Bedders rode into Lander to sell beef. It was on a bright clear day and many people were out on the street. Bedders felt their eyes on him immediately. He had been to town before but had seldom seen many people. The looks he got were not friendly.

The two restaurants in town already had contracts for beef. They coldly turned him away. There was a butcher shop in town, too. Bedders didn't think he would have much luck there, either, but took a deep breath and squared his shoulders as he started across the street. A sudden voice halted him.

'Mr Bedders?' Emily Patterson stood on the wooden boardwalk, her arms at her side awkwardly, as if she wasn't sure what to do with them.

Bedders hadn't realized he had come so close to the land office.

He stepped back on to the boardwalk and tipped his hat. 'Miss Patterson.'

'You've been to town three times this past month and you haven't stopped in to see me once.' A wisp of a smile was on her face. Her eyes were much larger and brighter than he remembered.

'Did you expect me to?'

For a moment her eyes clouded with darkness, but it passed quickly. 'I thought you might want to. If only to tell my father how foolish I was that day.'

'Foolish? For shooting at me? Or for missing?'

'Maybe a little of both,' she said. Her eyes flashed again with a hint of anger that faded. 'Really, I am sorry. I don't know what came over me.'

Bedders nodded. 'It's forgotten. Cavanaugh is a friend, right? You were looking out for him.'

Disappointment registered on her face and stayed there. 'Mr Cavanaugh is a friend of my father's.'

42

'I see.' Now it was Bedders who didn't know what to do with his hands.

'I understand you're trying to sell beef in town.'

'Not much luck there.'

'No. There's more than enough beef in this country, Mr Bedders. You might be able to sell some hides, but steak is one thing we've plenty of.' Bedders winced at the mention of hides. Emily noticed and asked, 'Did you lose many head?'

'About fifty.'

Emily shook her head. 'That valley will be hard to graze a steady herd. It's mostly been used by Cavanaugh and others as a holding area or a place to catch strays.'

'I've seen that herd of yor'n,' a voice said from behind. Bedders turned to find two Cavanaugh men, Lincoln and a shorter fellow with sharp features and small eyes and a cruel twist to his mouth. Grinning, Lincoln kept his big hands clear of the toy-sized guns strapped to his hips. 'Tain't nothin' but strays,' said Lincoln.

'What do you mean by that??'

Emily stepped forward and spoke softly, 'Lincoln, please.'

'Just being neighbourly, Emily.' His voice wasn't so taunting when he spoke to her. But he was not about to abandon what he had started.

Others in the street had heard the exchange and paused to watch. An air of expectation hung over the group. Lincoln, with one foot up on the walk and another in the hard-packed street, the long stretch of his legs allowing him to lean casually against a post, chewed on a toothpick at the corner of his mouth. The other man, about Bedders' height but bulkier, stood squarely on the walk, feet spread slightly, hands held loosely at his side. This man wore only one gun, but for his kind one would be enough. Bedders was being backed into a corner. He knew instinctively that he could not outdraw the man.

'It was a tough winter, wasn't it?' asked Lincoln. 'Sure it was. Folks around here lost more cattle than usual. Oh, not so many really. A couple hundred head. Just enough to get your attention, isn't that right, Jimmy?'

The shorter man nodded but never took his eyes off of Bedders.

'Never found the carcasses, though,' the other man added.

'This is Jimmy Christopher,' introduced Lincoln. Bedders glanced away from Christopher and saw the goading look in Lincoln's malevolent eyes. 'Hired him on this spring. He's real good chasing down strays.'

Ignoring the introduction, Christopher said, 'Cows just up and disappeared. Older ones with grown over brands.'

'Ride out to my range and take a look,' Bedders said. 'I lost fifty head last winter myself.'

'I've been to your range,' Christopher said. 'You and your partner've got more cows than you came into this country with.'

'He's not my partner.'

'You're a liar.' Christopher spoke the words slowly and clearly and just loud enough for them to hear.

It took all his might for Bedders not to draw on the man. It was what Christopher was waiting for. 'No. I'm not. Meagan and I split up the valley and the herd when we arrived. We're each of us on our own.'

'Birds of a feather,' said Christopher, a cruel grin on his face.

Lincoln laughed. 'He's a scrappy fellow, ain't he?'

Emily's hand touched Bedders' forearm. He stiffened

44

noticeably and with such suddenness that she gasped. Christopher made just the slightest sharp move, enough to show what he was thinking, wanting nothing more than to draw against Bedders. Then something in Christopher's eyes changed. He unbuckled his gunbelt and let it drop to the walk.

'I don't like you,' he said then drove a sudden fist into Bedders' jaw. The blow sent Bedders tumbling. He slammed against Emily's shoulder, knocking her down, a pile of blue calico on the boardwalk.

Lincoln shoved past both men and bent over the girl. 'Stop them, Lincoln,' she commanded, sweeping hair out of her eyes.

'Why?' Now that he saw she wasn't hurt the malevolent grin creased his face again.

'Because you started it.'

Bedders hadn't heard a word of what they said. He stood and unbuckled his own belt then jumped at Christopher. He caught another right in the side of his face, tumbling down the steps into the street. Rolling to his feet he blocked another haymaker then jabbed out with his blocking hand, crunching Christopher's nose. Blood spurted like a popping bladder.

Bedders stepped forward and threw a right-left-right combination, two to the body and one to the face. Christopher stumbled but managed to keep his wits about him even as his head began to swim. He scrambled away from Bedders on unsteady legs, catching hold of a hitching post then pushed off the wooden bar and threw himself at the rangy redhead. Bedders swung again but the ranch hand got in under the fist and slammed his heavy body into the youth.

They tumbled to the ground, kicking up dust and drawing an excited crowd. Grappling hand to hand, Christopher brought a knee up just missing Bedders' groin but hitting his thigh, causing a sharp, pinching pain. Bedders yelped, shoving Christopher away, then got to his feet. Christopher was on him again in an instant.

Bedders had a free hand now and drove a heavy fist into Christopher's gut. The man gasped with a violent intake of wind and staggered back. Limping a little, Bedders pursued and drove fists into the man's face, two, three, four times, until Christopher bled from a split lip and a cut over the left eye. The man dropped to both knees and slumped forward, exhausted.

Lincoln stepped down into the street and stood with hands on his hips, openly admiring the result.

'Better than I expected from you,' he said, pulling Christopher to his feet. The man's hat had come off during the fight. Lincoln scooped it up and put it none too gently on Christopher's head.

'Of course,' said Lincoln, 'your partner's got other men to do his fighting.'

'I told you he's not my partner.' Breathless, Bedders stepped back to the boardwalk and leaned against a post. Like a wary animal he watched Lincoln with great care.

'How's he paying for them hands?' Christopher asked. Dirty and bleeding and humiliated the man was coiled with hatred. 'Men cost money.'

'I don't know,' Bedders said, running his eyes up and down Christopher. 'You look cheap.'

Christopher's reaction was immediate. He leapt for Bedders, a growl in his throat, fists balled. Bedders had been ready. He met him and shoved a balled fist into the man's gut. Christopher crumpled to the ground with a groan.

Lincoln's expression changed now. His face was like stone.

'You don't want to push Cavanaugh men,' he said. 'We push back. Hard.'

Bedders thought to say something but held his tongue. He watched as Lincoln gathered Christopher to his feet and shoved him on to the boardwalk and down into a saloon. It was only after the two men entered the saloon that Bedders relaxed and turned toward Emily. She was standing there holding his gunbelt. She had loosed the thin rawhide strap from around the hammer and had her hand on the gun butt, ready to draw.

'They were looking for a fight,' she said, handing Bedders his gun and belt.

The redhead laughed. 'I guess that's right!'

She bent and picked up his hat from the boardwalk, brushing away the dust with her hand. She dented the peak again with some care before handing it back to him.

'Come along. I think I can find a buyer for some of your hides, if they're in any shape.'

He went with her across the street and down a few blocks to a tailor named Baclova, a pudgy-faced old man with wide moustaches and apple-red cheeks. He was another friend of the family and promised to give a fair price on the hides if they could be used. Bedders thanked the man and said he would bring them in the next day.

'I should be going back to the office now,' Emily said.

They were standing on the boardwalk near Bedders' horse. He had noticed a red mark on her cheek but hadn't been able to bring himself to ask about it. Finally the draw of it was too much for him and he found himself reaching up to touch it, a move that surprised them both.

'Did I give you that?' he asked.

She put a hand to her cheek, where he had almost touched it. 'I think this is more Mr Christopher's doing.'

Bedders nodded, not trusting himself to say what he thought about Christopher. He stepped into the street and climbed up into the saddle.

'I hope to see you again, Mr Bedders. Under more congenial circumstances.'

About to turn and ride away, Bedders paused, trying to give his thoughts time to form. 'You were ready to draw on them with my gun back there,' he finally said. 'Why?'

Emily stepped close to the rail. 'If Lincoln had joined in it wouldn't't've been a fair fight.'

'He wasn't going to join in. He was too worried about you.'

Luckily his horse knew the way home because Bedders was blind to everything on the ride back to the valley. His thoughts were in turmoil, wondering about Emily. She had tried to kill him not so long ago, a hotheaded mistake to be sure. But she had shot at him. Today she was ready to draw a gun to defend him. She was the prettiest thing he had seen in a month of Sundays, and was surely the most beautiful woman in Lander, at least to his liking. Meagan had seen it right off, and it was no secret now that Lincoln had it bad for the girl. And Cavanaugh? A man old enough to be her father? Did she have feelings for him? Best to steer clear of her altogether, he decided. There were too many men who had first claim. Bedders had enough trouble of his own, he didn't need to borrow someone else's.

The next morning Bedders divided the supplies in the shanty and brought his share to his cabin. He yet needed a table and chairs and a cupboard and so began drawing plans up in his mind to build them. Fresh water was no problem, though. A while back he had discovered another small creek that ran along the base of the northern slope just below his cabin. The outhouse was another matter. That he had built some distance from the cabin.

The cows had spread out some over the past few days, a handful of them bunching at the rocks at the far end of the valley. Bedders was about to ride out and chouse them back toward fresh grass when he spotted riders coming. At first he thought it was Meagan and his men returning, but they crossed the creek and rounded Apple Rock, nothing but dark pinpricks against the golden land. Eventually, he could make out the large form and grey-blond head of Amos Cavanaugh sitting regally atop a blood red mare. Two hard looking men rode beside him.

Something about their look sent a wave of uneasiness through Bedders. He reached into the cabin and pulled his Remington down off a peg and stepped forward to greet the men.

CHAPTER FOUR

Amos Cavanaugh trotted up to the top of the plateau then slowed to a walk before stopping fifty feet from Bedders, his two men acting in concert. Neither of them said anything, they just watched Bedders and the rifle in his hands. Cavanaugh nodded to Bedders then slowly turned his head to look about the valley. He had seen the set-up riding in: the shanty leaning with neglect and Meagan's new home, Bedders' new cabin, the cattle grazing, more on one side of the creek than the other. Quick understanding flashed in his eyes.

'You boys seem to be doing fairly well,' he said. 'You may even have a few more head than you came with.'

With the hundred head Meagan had taken to sell the range now supported about four hundred and fifty cows.

'Anything south of the creek belongs to Meagan,' Bedders told him.

Cavanaugh nodded. 'Heard you fellas had a falling out.'

'Not really. He just needs to do this on his own.'

Cavanaugh was looking deeply at Bedders now, reading the young man's face and understanding the fuller meaning of his words.

'Then I guess you're having some trouble. Lost a few head.'

'About fifty.'

'It was a hard winter for some other folks, too. Some of them lost fifty or so head.'

Bedders realized his jaw was hurting from clenching it so tightly. He didn't want to have to fight Cavanaugh, too.

Nodding toward the rock pit further down the valley Bedders said, 'I've got the bones and hides to prove it.'

'Mind if I step down?' Cavanaugh smiled, or something like it cracked his crusty face.

Bedders thought on that a moment. He did not want to be enemies with this man. He wanted to be let alone enough to make a go of his small ranch. He should have known better, he told himself. Come on to a range and people will get suspicious. They'll shoot at you and pick fights and ride up to your door to intimidate you. He wondered if he hadn't been better off just a rolling tumbleweed.

'What do you want?'

Cavanaugh fidgeted in his saddle but did not attempt to climb down uninvited. 'I understand you and Jimmy Christopher had a dust up.'

Cavanaugh's men grinned at the mention of the fight in town yesterday.

'Lincoln ought to keep him on a shorter leash.' That got a chuckle out of the men. Even the big rancher ducked his head away to hide a grin.

'Well,' Cavanaugh said, 'Lincoln has his uses. But you won't see Christopher around these parts again.' Bedders couldn't keep surprise from registering on his face. 'I'd like to talk to you about something. I have a proposal I'd like you to hear.'

Bedders said, 'Step down.'

Cavanaugh got down and stretched. He looked on the small cabin admiringly, walking to it and slapping the sides of it.

'I began with less than this. Built it myself, too, though not so well. More like that shanty you first built. That thing brings back memories.' He sucked in a deep breath, taking in the entire range. 'Had the whole country before me in those days, just me and a couple hands. Held off a few Indians, and more than a few rustlers.' He shook his head, nostalgia threatening to sweep over him. Bedders watched him, his rifle lowered, forgetting about the other two. 'Could've used a hand back in those days. Never got one. That's what I'm offering you.'

'I don't understand.'

'My land's too big to take too many of the hands away from it for a length of time. So I need other men, capable men to help me do a job.'

'And that is?'

'Trail drivin', son! What other job is there?' Now that he wasn't scolding or barking, Cavanaugh seemed marvellously cheerful. 'I've got three herds I'm buying down in Garden City in a week. I'll need help driving them up. I'll pay your way down on the train, including passage for your horse. You help me drive 'em back I'll give you fifty prime head. Your herd could stand some new stock.'

Bedders agreed. 'But I can pay my own way down, and bring my own grub. I'll help you drive them steers for a hundred and fifty head.'

Cavanaugh looked over to his men, standing by their horses. They looked expectant and not a little fearful. The large rancher's face had gone red and then a great gush of laughter burst forth. The sound made everyone jump.

'Hell, boy, no one brings their own food on my drives. You'll eat what everyone else eats. But if you pay your own way down and stick with the drive you'll earn your one hundred and fifty. You'll be gone about a month. Can you be ready in three days; we're meeting in Rawlins.'

Bedders cast a glance down on to his range. 'What about my spread?'

'I'm leaving plenty of boys behind. I'll have them ride in once in a while and check up on things.'

He didn't have to think long before accepting the offer. 'I'll be in Rawlins to meet you.' They shook, one single, powerful pump of their clasped hands, but it had the feel of permanence to it. Like it was set in granite.

Bedders returned to Lander the next day, bringing the leather hides he had salvaged. The tailor, Emil Jaeger, took a long time looking them over then sent Bedders away for an hour.

Fiddlefooting around town, he bought another canteen and stopped to have his knife sharpened. He bought a few boxes of cartridges for his Colt's revolver and for the Remington. Purposely he avoided the land office but found himself there anyway, ready to scratch at the door like a kitten. Mr Patterson saw him through the dusty pane and waved him in.

John Patterson was a beefy man from the waist up, but his legs were frail and spindly. He sat in a wooden Colson wheelchair with a slatted seat and back. His arms were powerful enough to push the creaking chair with ease despite his bulk. He had a friendly face with large, round eyes.

'Don't hang around on the walk, son. Come in,' he said.

Bedders shut the door, a bell tinkling overhead. Behind

the counter, at the back of the narrow room, a black curtain parted and Emily stepped out. She stopped short, then smiled broadly.

'Twice in one week,' she said. Damn the girl, Bedders thought. She was always so quick-witted and coy. 'This is a honour.'

'I came to sell my hides. Mr Jaeger is looking them over now.'

Emily noticed the packages in his hand. Her eyes widened at the site of rifle and pistol cartridges and her face paled slightly.

'I'm leaving the valley for a bit,' he told her, setting his packages on the counter. 'About a month.'

'Driving?' Patterson asked.

'Yes, sir. For Mr Cavanaugh. He's moving a herd up from Garden City and he needs an extra hand. I'll get cattle for wages.'

'I'm glad,' Emily said as she stepped up to the counter.

'Because I'm leaving?'

She smiled. 'Because you're going with Mr Cavanaugh.'

'Good man, Amos. You stick with him, he's a good neighbour. Just steer clear of some of his men. Couple of them are just plain ornery.'

'Dad, Mr Bedders had a run-in with Jimmy Christopher yesterday.' There was a glow of pride in her bearing suddenly, and she smiled at him again.

'Heard about that. Cleaned his clock for him, or so a little bird told me.' He glanced up at his daughter then back to Bedders. 'You watch him, son. He's a mean cuss.'

'Mr Cavanaugh said he fired him yesterday.'

Bedders had his hands on the counter, loosely beside his packages. Emily placed a hand over his. 'That is good news,' she told him.

'I'll be gone a month,' Bedders said after a few moments.

'You said that, son.'

Emily smiled. 'A month's not so long.'

Bedders hastily took his leave, promising to stop in for dinner when he returned. Emily walked him to the door and wouldn't let him leave until he yielded to her invitation. Back at the tailor's shop Jaeger gave him a fair price for the hides, even though a few of them weren't good for much more than scraps. With his heavy accent he made it clear that Emily had come by and spoken to him on Bedders' behalf. She had also ordered a leather vest, specifically requesting Jaeger use the hides the young rancher had brought in.

There was little time to wonder about Emily, though. If he meant to ride with Cavanaugh he had to hurry. Still, the thought of her lingered in his mind as he returned home to pack his saddlebags. Loping out of the valley the following day, the image of her soft face haunted him. For miles he carried an uneasy feeling with him, as if he was leaving behind something important.

Excitement kept him from sleeping well that night. He tossed and turned, even though he was usually more comfortable sleeping under the stars than under a roof. He thought of Emily but now, with miles and time behind him, other thoughts entered his mind. The uneasiness he felt earlier had stayed with him.

He was putting a lot of trust in a man that he did not know. Trusting that Cavanaugh would have his men watch his herd and not steal them. That he was a hard man was undeniable. But he seemed honest and fair. Hell, Bedders thought, more than fair. One hundred and fifty head of cattle in payment for a month's work. It didn't make a lot of sense unless the rancher meant to steal Bedders' herd then renege on his promise. If he did that, Bedders would be ruined. He couldn't fight Cavanaugh and the kind of men he employed.

That he would hire men like Lincoln and Christopher was to be expected. To hold the size of range he had, to control such a large business he would need strong men. Cruel men, too, if occasion called for it. Yet he had fired Christopher. Bedders wondered if that was because of the fight in town, or if Christopher had more such sins on his tally sheet. Probably a lot more, Bedders thought.

By mid-afternoon the next day Bedders had reached Muddy Gap Pass and began the climb up the narrow, well-worn trail. Big leafy black alder and bushy dark green and silvery juniper formed a broken canopy over the trail. A trickling stream cut slightly below the trail, covered with ferns and grass and clogged with mossy rocks. Further into the forest were glossy-leafed ash, hackberry, and chokecherry trees. Dappled sunlight fell on the trail and all around him.

Absently, the sound of woodpeckers attacking a tree rose in his consciousness above the soporific babbling of the stream and the croaking of frogs and the peeping of a hundred birds. It was an angry sound, Bedders thought, looking around for its source. Then it got louder – a creaking, rending sound – and he realized woodpeckers were not making the noise.

Reining his piebald, Bedders glanced about him, a hand on the pistol at his hip. He did not usually ride with a gun strapped on but the lingering uneasiness had made him wary.

The cracking sound got louder just before he spotted a lodgepole pine tumbling toward him. The narrow path offered no cover. With a kick of his spurs, he and the piebald jumped down into the creekbed. The horse stumbled on the moss-covered rocks. Bedders used that momentum to fall the horse, wrenching the animal's neck with the reins.

They landed in soft mud and underbrush just as the tree cracked through the forest and smashed itself on the trail. Great shards and splinters came flying off the trunk in a deadly explosion. Knife-sharp chunks of the tree whistled over Bedders' head, slicing into the underbrush and embedding in the trunks of nearby trees.

The piebald was stunned for a moment, letting out a low groan. For a fearful moment Bedders thought the animal had broken a leg. But it got to its feet on shaky, tentative legs, then bolted up the side of the creekbed to the trail. Trying to stand Bedders felt a sharp pain in his thigh just above the knee. An old broken branch, part of it crumbling with decay, had stabbed him through his woollen pant leg. The wound bled profusely, but it wasn't deep. He took a moment, keeping his eyes up toward the trail, to clean the gash with his neckerchief before he climbed to higher ground.

Bedders had his pistol out now. The tree falling could have been an accident, but he didn't think so. He had just climbed over a shattered section of the tree when a shot rang out and splashed wood chips over him.

He threw himself to the ground, rolling to a rock for cover, as another shot zipped overhead. A third shot followed him. And then silence. Bedders had seen the briefest flare of gunfire as he rolled. The shooter was two hundred feet further up the hill and a hundred feet off the trail.

A few feet from the rock was a box elder with a fairly

wide trunk. Bedders got behind this and rose to his feet. No shots came. Caution slowing his steps, Bedders moved around the tree and started climbing the hill. The many trees and thick underbrush helped to hide him, but they also made the going noisy.

Several more shots rang out, cracking through branches. Bedders spotted the muzzle flash and returned fire. Running up the hill, he threw himself behind another large tree trunk, reloaded, then fired again. He could hear the rustling of leaves and the sickly creaking of rotting branches as the gunman moved. Bedders peeked around the protective trunk and saw a flutter of movement in the forest. Then he heard the clop of horse hoofs galloping away.

It took nearly two hours for Bedders to clear away enough of the fallen tree to pass. He had tried to lead the piebald around it but its roots had been embedded in a steep hillside that neither he nor the horse could climb.

Following the shooter's trail was simple. The man did not once veer off the Muddy Gap Pass trail. His horse was shod with common enough shoes that had a tiny diamond design that left an imprint. Once out of the Gap the trail was still clear enough. But the ground got harder and eventually all horse sign disappeared.

Bedders stopped at a stagecoach way station and paid the caretaker for supper, some bandages, a needle and thread for his pants, and oats for his horse. The caretaker had seen no one that day, no lone rider or coach, which was due in two days' time, and he was hungry for conversation.

For his part Bedders was anxious to move on. He knew he couldn't identify the shooter, and didn't think the man would be coming back for him. But he wanted to get to

Rawlins. The caretaker offered a cot, though, and a place to sleep that was safer than the open range, so he stayed and spent long hours talking with the man. So pleased was the caretaker that the next morning's breakfast was thrown in for free.

Bedders arrived in Rawlins that evening and took a room at the Indian Hotel, boarding his horse next door. The next morning he went down to the railroad station, asking around for Cavanaugh. The big man was not hard to miss. He had perched himself on top of several crates and was directing the chaotic traffic milling around a blackened, smoking Union Pacific locomotive. Dozens of horses were being loaded into slatted boxcars, along with a chuck wagon, and a dozen saddles.

A red-faced powerhouse of a man with gigantic fore-arms bellowed to the railroad men to be careful with the chuck wagon. A gaggle of drovers stood around hazing the crew as they struggled with the ungainly thing.

Bedders led his horse to box cars and found the wran-gler, a skinny youth with a long face and watery, bloodshot eyes. He introduced himself and handed the piebald over to him.

Cavanaugh nodded only a brief acknowledgement of Bedders, his mind on the circus of activity he was super-vising. A few of the hands came up to him and they shook then climbed aboard and found seats.

The ride was pleasant enough once they got moving. The train creaked and groaned its way out of Rawlins amid dust and heat. At full speed, though, with the windows pulled down, the car was comfortable, although noisy.

That didn't matter to the drovers. They were noisier. Raucous stories were told, a pint bottle began making the rounds, and anyone not tied down and with their eyes front became victim of some hazing. The train took them to Cheyenne then south to Denver then east. With water stops and a break to let another train pass, it took a day and a half to reach their destination.

After the noise of the train, the relative calm and quiet of the prairie seemed grave-like. Man and horse had piled out of the train cars, nervous energy powering them, each anxious to take to the trail. They were all settled now ten miles from town, a swollen summer sun just beginning to dip below the dry, flat land. Three thousand cattle mewled quietly in the gathering dark.

The task of what lay ahead was on no man's mind that night. The pint bottle had been taken away by the red-faced cook, but the conversation was just as spirited as it had been on the train. Word had gotten around about how Bedders had bloodied Christopher in Lander, and the hands all laughed about that. Christopher's loss to the outfit was not a big one. He was razzed about trying to take on Lincoln, too, and for a moment Bedders thought he would have to fight one or two of the men. But these were not ornery men. They could poke fun, and have it poked back at them, but fighting was something they took on seriously.

At some point during the evening, Bedders became one of them.

Bedders had ridden many trails and worked every end of a drive. They put him on drag, which was fair since he was the new hand. Experience had taught him how to minimize the amount of dust he breathed in. After a few days he was rotated to swing. Cavanaugh was testing him.

Two weeks passed as they made their way out of Kansas, across the northeastern corner of Colorado and the South Platte, and back into Wyoming near Pine Bluffs. The work was hard and the days long, but it satisfied Bedders and although dead tired and bone achy he was happy.

The sliver of a quarter moon was spinning across a black sky when Bedders came into camp after his turn riding circle on the sleeping herd. They had bed down the cows late that day because toward evening they had come on to water and the animals drank their fill. Cavanaugh didn't want to make camp when the beeves had bellies full of water so they drove on another few miles. Everyone was exhausted that night.

Bedders got a plate of beans and bacon and sourdough biscuits and huddled up next to a small rock to eat. Some of the other hands were still awake, but most had gone to sleep anticipating their turn at guarding the herd. Bedders had just settled into his bedroll when Cavanaugh rose and went to the edge of the camp, head cocked, listening, firelight dancing on his back.

'They're on the move,' he said.

'Stampede?' someone asked, edgily.

'No. But they're moving just the same. Everybody up.' He said it quietly but every hand was instantly on his feet. Standing there in absolute silence, not even breathing, Bedders could hear the shuffling sound of hoofs on dirt. It was very faint. The cattle were mewling, too, grunting with annoyance. 'Mount up. And pull out your guns.'

Bedders went for his horse.

'Not you,' Cavanaugh called, stopping him in mid-stride. 'You help Cook with the wagon.' There was an edge to the rancher's voice. Fuming, Bedders turned toward the man. If the other hands had heard Cavanaugh, they ignored him as they bustled around him getting to their horses. 'I'm one of the hands, ain't I?'

'Yes.' Bedders expected Cavanaugh to look angry, or

suspicious. He was the new man and the rancher had made veiled comments about somebody new rustling cattle in the area. But Cavanaugh's frown came more from worry, or maybe pity, than anything else, and this confused him.

'Then I'm riding with the others,' Bedders told him, and turned for his horse. Within minutes he was aboard the piebald, pistol strapped to his side.

The trail boss, a man named Aguilar who had one dead eye and was as grizzly as an old mossy horn, and just about as ornery, gave instructions to the hands to circle the herd wary for night riders. 'Don't be shootin' at shadows, ya lunkheads. You'll start the whole blamed mess of 'em running.' There were wooded hills to the east, he reminded, and a cut through them. 'If rustlers have gotten into the herd that's where they'd take 'em,' he said.

Bedders rode with one of the other hands south around the herd, walking their horses and squinting at the darkness. The other rider, Randon, pulled up, stretching an arm out to touch Bedders. Leaning close, Randon said, 'I see something.' He was pointing into the grey-black mass of mewling cows. The animals were getting more restless by the minute. If there was something in with them, Bedders could not see it. Randon pulled away and, drawing his gun, nudged his horse and waded in.

Bedders rode on, sweeping around the herd toward the eastern hills. The sounds of moving cattle were louder here. The animals were nervous. Like a tinderbox any spark would ignite them. The piebald fidgeted as well, infected by the disquietude.

There was a flow to their movement. Bedders and the piebald were caught up in it, bumping and being bumped by cattle. The horse was beginning to shake, penned in as it was. Bedders' palms began to sweat. Gently, he urged the horse out of the stream and up the side of hill that appeared suddenly out of the darkness. They climbed for a few minutes leaving behind the stream of cattle.

Bedders dismounted and worked his way through the trees over to the cut slope. There was barely enough moonlight to see pale glimpses of the cows entering the cut below. A flash of something white caught his eye and he froze. Scanning slowly with his eyes, Bedders searched the hillside. It took a moment for him to realize what he was seeing. A shirt sparkling just for a second in the slender moonlight.

From this vantage point Bedders could just make out two other riders below the hill, each working a flank on a bunch culled from the main herd. There may have been five hundred head in that bunch moving almost silently through the cut in the hills. The man with the white shirt in the trees above them was positioned as lookout. He'd provide cover if the others were accosted, or maybe start a stampede.

Bedders holstered his pistol and pulled off his boots then started down the hill using the trees for cover. Each step he took was a delicate thing. He used great care not to crack a twig or crackle some leaves. The man with the white shirt leaned out from behind a tree and waved down at the others. Bedders froze, hoping he was as difficult to see as they were.

The cattle were entering the cut when Bedders moved again. He drew his pistol and stuck it in the back of the rustler.

'You don't want to make a sound, friend,' he said.

A thrill of surprise rippled through the rustler and he jerked, wanting to strike out. Good sense froze him. Then someone fired a shot down among the cattle and a great roar rose up as the animals bawled and started running. The sound distracted Bedders. Seeing his moment, the rustler spun and swung a heavy fist into Bedders' face even as he swatted the pistol aside. Bedders fired involuntarily. A gash opened on his cheek from the rustler's blow and he tumbled sideways, smashing into a tree trunk.

A call went out across the valley, men hawing the cattle, urging them to stop. Even as they did that, shots were fired, scaring the animals even more.

Bedders struck back at the rustler, swinging with his gunhand, catching the man's shoulder. A round left caught the man's face and he tumbled to the ground and rolled down the hill a few feet. Bedders couldn't see the rustler well at all, didn't know if he was drawing a gun or raising a hand. Suddenly something whizzed by his head and landed with a *thunk!* in the tree trunk beside him. Bedders didn't look at it. He fired at that glowing white shirt. But the rustler had moved and the shot missed.

Crouching low Bedders crept through the trees waiting for a hand to grab him or a bullet to find him. Below the herd was still streaming through the cut. He couldn't see any of the riders now, not even Cavanaugh's men. Then he saw a flash of white, heard a gunshot and a bullet snapped through thin branches. Bedders returned fire until the white shirt vanished.

They spent two days rounding up the herd, another day resting them. None of the men had been hurt but they had killed one of the rustlers. In the light of day no one recognized him. Bedders had taken his turn viewing the body, dreading it. He expected the man to be one of the hands hired by Meagan, but he wasn't. Relief flooded through him then he tensed seeing Cavanaugh watching him.

Bedders took Cavanaugh into the hills to show him where he had seen the white-shirt rustler. The rancher took in the scene quietly, nodding. The tip of a knife was buried in a tree trunk and Bedders figured that was what the rustler had thrown at him. Its glistening point had barely missed his head.

Cavanaugh pulled it out of the tree and looked it over. There was no recognition in his eyes. 'Here,' he said, handing it to Bedders. 'Man could always use a good knife.'

Taking the knife, Bedders saw that it was common enough with a plain walnut hilt, shorter than a Bowie, but well balanced. On casual inspection, there was nothing about it to give away the owner's identity. Yet, looking at it closely Bedders' heart sank. There was a gouge at the base of the blade like a Spanish notch where more than a year ago on the trail up from Texas the blade had been chipped being used to open a can of peaches.

CHAPTER FIVE

Meagan waited in a buggy outside the land office. He wore a new suit of clothes, with new boots and hat, the picture of a gentleman caller. He had been waiting some fifteen minutes. Absently, his fingers drummed on the cushioned black button seat. He wondered idly how ridiculous he looked in a stiff collar and shining hat. Such clothes he had never worn in his life. He had spent most of his days in dungarees, a poor man's pant he had come to loathe. But wages from a dry goods store were not enough to buy the kind of clothes boys like Bedders took to.

Boys, he scoffed in his mind. He had stopped being a boy very soon after Bedders had left. Abandoned him, really. Fast friends but so different. Oh, the thrill he would get watching Bedders hop on a strange horse and start to ride. The animal invariably bucked at the light weight on its back, but the youngster always seemed to enjoy it. Even when he was thrown. Such lies Meagan would tell. He laughed now, remembering them, attracting more curiosity from people on the street. Let them look. Damn it, he'd laugh if he wanted to.

He told Gregson that one time that the horse saw a snake and bolted even though Bedders had done all he could to calm the animal. Of course, Bedders had tried to ride the jittery beast. A dozen good horsemen had tried to ride the animal the previous week and none could. Gregson had made a handful betting against the blustery, prideful drovers. But Bedders thought he could do better. He always thought he could. Not that time, though. Gregson hadn't believed the lie and cuffed the both of them before he threw them out. Not too many days later Bedders rode out of town leaving Meagan behind, branded a liar.

Things had gotten hard, then. He had a drunken father who had no time for him and a mother who hated the west and, thankfully, ran off after another year. He was orphaned the following year when his father wandered out into the desert drunk and was never seen again. The pastor wanted nothing to do with him after Bedders ran off so Meagan kicked around town, earning his keep and a few pennies more. Eventually he was absorbed into Parmenter's family and set to work in the general store. It was a comfortable, if joyless existence, and Meagan thought he would end his days there without ever having really tasted life.

Then Bedders returned and the world opened to him. His brash friend, with whom he'd parted badly but made up with in letters, was even brasher than he had been years before. He was wild-eyed. He found Avalon, he had said, a place of such incomparable beauty that he couldn't bear to be in it alone. He had to share it with his best friend.

Meagan had cried that night, filled with joy and over-whelming relief. He would live now. All along the trail north Bedders had regaled him with stories of the drover's life. Bandits and whiskey and wrestling and shooting matches, and women. Oh, the women he talked about from towns all over.

He had never mentioned hard work, though. It was all a joy to him. And it came easily.

The talk made Meagan's blood boil. So many years he had wasted chained to a broom handle, nothing more than a grocery clerk. One night on the trail under a black sky he looked at the guileless, angelic face of his sleeping friend, with firelight dancing deviltry into his features, and wanted to ask Bedders why he'd never thought to take him along when he left Spearman. Why he had just left him behind.

That's when the hate began. The hate for the life he was forced to lead, for his useless parents, for the pinched and lemon-faced Parmenter and his ugly daughters – and for his friend.

He had a lot to make up for. A lot of time, a lot of money, a lot of whiskey, a lot of shooting. And a lot of women.

'I'm sorry,' Emily said. She stood beside the buggy, appearing there as if by magic. Startled, Meagan jumped out of his seat to help her in. 'I didn't mean to take so long,' she said.

Meagan put a smile on his face and said, 'I was daydreaming. I'm sure it wasn't that long.'

She took his hand and stepped up into the buggy. Meagan ran around to the other side and climbed in. He took the reins, hitching them lightly and calling to the horse. Meagan kept the horse to a slow walk, wanting everyone in town to see him with Emily.

'At this pace we won't be back before tomorrow,' she told him. Her eyes were bright and kind and she smiled at him.

'Daydreaming again.' He hitched the horse into a light trot.

They left town following the road north toward Milford, past a few houses and several groves of apple trees. There was a turn-off before Milford that looped around and up a little into the foothills of the Wind River Range. The low hills were filled with brown grass and the sporadic colour of fall foliage dotted with the occasional green of a pinion or bristlecomb pine, or a larch that had yet to shed its needles. The sun lay like a warm blanket over them, with just a hint of a cool breeze in the air.

Meagan circled the loop, passing an old, overgrown and rutted road that went up into the hills to the abandoned gold mines. Ahead was a small clearing with a large golden willow set inside it, a little off-centre which provided a dappled canopy of shade. Meagan stopped the buggy.

'It's lovely,' Emily said, looking around. 'I've not been up this way.'

Meagan helped her down then fetched a picnic basket from the rear of the buggy and a thick blanket.

'I've had occasion to ride around some. I've seen all sorts of beautiful things.' He beamed at her, melting into the liquid beauty of her eyes.

As Meagan busied himself with the blanket and basket, Emily went to a tree and began picking apples, piling a couple of handfuls into the bib of her dress. Without preamble she began eating one.

'Careful you don't get a stomach ache,' Meagan warned.

'Oh, these aren't crab apples. They're moose apples.' She laughed brightly at the strange look that blossomed on his face.

'Folks tend to think any kind of apple mentioned in connection with an animal as coming from the back end of the critter and not fit to eat,' he told her, choosing words for a lady's ears.

'Well, these are sweet.' She tossed him one as she sat on the blanket. 'Folks call them moose apples because they stay on the trees until after the snow flies and the moose come down out of the hills to eat them. They're a little tart yet.'

Meagan took a bite and nodded his satisfaction.

Dinner had been prepared by one of the restaurants in town, and its warm smells lifted out of the basket. Meagan laid it out, giving a china plate to Emily and a thick cloth napkin. He pulled the cork on a bottle of wine, too, but poured very little into a glass for her and not much more for himself. They ate and talked about little things for a while, not saying much. Emily had agreed to the outing because Meagan had been so persistent and earnest. He was a nice enough fellow but something about him made her uneasy. She felt she would be safe enough on a picnic, though. Meagan wasn't one to explode, or so she believed. The trouble in him was taking its time bubbling to the surface.

He had come to town many times since his arrival in the valley and had always made a point to stop in and say hello. She had been courteous to him, even a little friendly. She recognized immediately his intent and his desire, and she steered a course around both. Still he persisted, using friendly chatter and a disarming smile to weaken her resolve.

He had tried to kiss her once, but she had manoeuvred well and left him with his lips almost touching a rather warm stove chimney. He hadn't tried that again.

'I think it's good for a man to travel, to explore. It rounds him out, educates him,' she told him.

'Burns the wild out of him, too, I imagine.'

'Yes, that's true.'

'I ain't been no place. Not really. Never left home until me and Nix came north with our little herd. 'Course now I can't get enough of riding. I go out looking for all kinds of things.'

'Well, you certainly found this lovely spot.'

Meagan blushed at the compliment. He was quite unused to such talk from a woman. Parmenter's daughters were as dour as their mother, caring as little for conversation as they did for their appearance. For most of his life Meagan had been silent simply because no one would speak with him. It had given him a sullen disposition. In the company of Emily, though, his emotions were charged. A craving had been lit like a bonfire, threatening to consume him. It made him unsteady and uncertain with his words, and created a thick layer of frustration just below the thin veneer of confidence he tried to project.

They ate for a while in silence, Emily glad for the quiet. She found her mind wandering from the moment, fixing on other moments that seemed so real until she remembered that she had created them in her head. Moments with Carrot Bedders. Not for the first time had she wondered about that name. It couldn't be his real name. But then, it didn't matter, really. His face came to her mind's eye, smiling, which was strange because the man rarely did that. He had laughed that once, talking about Meagan getting beat up by Lincoln. She wondered for a moment if he had a cruel streak. But, no, he couldn't have, she thought with certainty. What was it about him that attracted her so? He wasn't necessarily handsome, though he had such strong shoulders and a narrow waist. That mop of red, curly hair had kept him looking young even though hard years in the saddle showed in his weathered face. His skin wasn't as cracked and leathery brown as Lincoln's or Mr Cavanaugh's, but it would be some day. She thought about that, of Bedders growing older, more leathery, and she smiled. He would still look young, she determined. His eyes with their joyful fire would keep him looking like a kid.

She found herself smiling and then felt Meagan's eyes on her.

'Has it been a good summer for you?' she asked, deflecting the curiosity in Meagan's face.

'Better for me than for Nix. I managed to round up some strays along with buying a cheap herd from a guy what needed the cash. Just brought 'em in last month.'

Emily decided to probe a little deeper. 'Why did you and Mr Bedders divide the valley? Do you mind my asking?'

'I don't mind.' He had been sitting across from her, the basket and laid out food between them. He scooted around that barrier now and settled close to her. 'Emily, I've got to have something of my own, something I can build with my own two hands. A place I can share with someone special and leave to children when I'm gone.' He had tried to reach out to her but Emily moved her hands away. It was a casual thing. She took the bowl of chicken and, wrapping the towel around the uneaten pieces, put it back in the hamper. The move had been done slowly, her eyes on Meagan attentively, so that the moment passed and he withdrew.

She had listened to him, he knew, with mild interest not desire. His jaw tightened.

'I'm sure you hear men talk like this all the time,' he said. There was a touch of bitterness in his voice.

'Not all the time, Abel.'

72

He noticed an icy edge to her voice. He realized what he had said and how it sounded. 'What I meant, Emily, was. . . .'

'I know what you meant.' There was sympathy in her eyes now.

'No. I only meant that you are very beautiful and that through no invitation by you men will speak to you this way because their hearts demand it.' He found he was suddenly breathless, and not a little amazed at the cogent thought he had spoken aloud. He felt he hadn't been making sense all afternoon, until he had spoken those words.

'I guess Nix and me aren't so different on that score,' he said.

She laughed pleasantly and asked, 'Why do you call him Nix?'

Meagan shook his head and smiled. 'He'd get in trouble a lot, ol' Carrot. Folks called him that because of his hair and it just kind of stuck. He wouldn't listen to anybody growing up. Least of all me. He'd be off to do something he shouldn't and I'd tell him he'd get a switch across his bottom if he didn't come back. He'd just smile at me and say nix. Heard it from him so often I took to calling him that.'

Meagan looked up to find Emily absorbing every word he was speaking. A blush came into her cheeks and she looked away.

Conversation died after that and soon they were back in the buggy heading back to Lander. Meagan had turned sullen and Emily could see resentment was bubbling just beneath his surface.

The grass was thinning.

Since returning from the Cavanaugh drive Bedders had

worked the cattle every day, spending hours in the saddle. Without barbed wire or other fencing, the cows would not stay where they were herded. Always they would wander, looking for new grass to eat. Bedders kept them bunched, creating paddocks in his mind. He'd let them eat the grass down then move them to the next area he had cordoned off in his head.

If this section of the valley had been as densely grown with grass as Meagan's side, he would have enough for his herd of three hundred and twenty head to graze all year round. But there had been many patches of empty hard-packed dirt dotted about his land, places in which grass had a hard time growing. A range that should support better than five hundred head wouldn't even serve his three hundred. He would lose more cattle this winter.

Upon his return, Bedders had been infused with energy and hope. The range looked inviting and green, and filled with his cattle the old image he once held of a healthy land teeming with cows sprang again to mind. Immediately, he had set to work clearing the scrub oak from about the range, salvaging it for kindling. Then he positioned the cattle, allowing their droppings to fertilize the barren soil. He knew very little about managing the land. For the most part he was guessing. But he had little to lose. In time some grass began to grow and Bedders became more encouraged.

Fall was on them now, though, and Bedders knew the grass that was sticking out of the ground and what would grow in the next six weeks before the rains came and made his end of the valley a sopping mess wouldn't be enough to last the winter. What he had worked for this spring and summer would be gone.

A directionless desperation filled him. It made him

anxious, but fired no clear thought as to what he should do.

At the other end of the valley Meagan seemed to be doing well. There was close to a thousand head in Meagan's Circle-M herd. Choice of that brand had caused some upset in the area, close as it was to Cavanaugh's Star-M. But Meagan's M was bigger and a star could not readily be made into circle. Meagan had pleaded ignorance and apologized but since he had branded the herd he didn't see how he could make a change without his cows looking like they had been stolen and re-branded. Meagan had smiled saying that but no one else had seen the humour.

Meagan's range looked better, too. This late in the year the grass, still fairly full and high, retained its vibrant colours. Yet Bedders wondered if there would be enough land to feed so many cows through the winter. Already Meagan had let part of the herd stray outside the valley and to the east toward 'Pistol' Nate Danelles' range. He had heard that some of Danelles' men had ridden close to Meagan's herd, glaring at the Circle-M riders, Glen Lefferts and Lloyd Baxter. An argument was brewing. Although no shots had been fired, talk was that it would come soon enough.

The soporific motion of his horse under him and the warm sun and cool breeze made Bedders drift in his saddle. He was rounding up the herd to move them to a new paddock, his mind wandering, flirting with sleep. Some days were filled with tedium.

Several of the cows had congregated in the northeast corner of the valley where the smaller stream trickled down into some rocks. There was a hump in the hills there where a patch of grass ducked behind a rise. Bedders had always managed to keep the cattle from wandering over to that corner but as he had been dozing he now saw a dozen head had gathered there.

He let the horse wander over in that direction, pausing occasionally to redirect one of the critters. He could tell the piebald was tired and he debated rounding up the strays in the corner. Hunger began to scratch at his belly like some ally cat. Lazy as he was feeling, though, he didn't think he'd come back on to this part of the range if he stopped now for something to eat. He'd probably just curl up on his home-made cot and take a nap.

Nudging the sluggish piebald forward he sighed heavily as they trotted toward the valley corner. But as he neared he noticed there were fewer than the dozen head he had seen just a few minutes ago. Then one cow went behind the hill followed by another and then a third. None of them came back out.

Bedders kicked his horse into a gallop, concern eating at him. He crossed at the small stream, noting that the water rounded the hill. Following it he saw that there was a grassy gap between the two steep sides of a sheer gorge wide enough for a score of cattle. The gap had been hidden by the hill hump, disguised as a dead end.

A thrill of excitement coursed through Bedders. He nudged the piebald forward, angling around the cows that were slowly making their way through the gorge. The land rose at a nearly imperceptible rate. The sheer rock sides were of weathered limestone and in places were stained red from iron deposits like Apple Rock.

The trail wound through the gorge for nearly a mile before it dipped and widened. An incredible vista opened to Bedders as he rode down out of the gorge, and for long minutes he sat in awe of what he had found.

Lloyd Baxter had been left alone in the valley with Meagan's growing herd while the boss was out cattin'.

Already a surly man, Baxter's temperament worsened the longer he stayed in his saddle. The other Circle-M rider, Glen Lefferts, was watching part of the herd outside the valley. They were crowding Danelles' range to the southeast and tempers were beginning to flare. Soon there would be gunplay, and that was fine with Baxter. Babysitting a bunch of mewling cows was not his idea of fun. Fun was women and whiskey and shooting. But you needed money for that, and Meagan had a way for them all to get what they needed.

Baxter snarled out a short laugh at the thought of Meagan. Upon meeting the dude for the first time there hadn't been much to recommend him. He wore the wrong clothes for a drover, was too thin, and he had the scheming eyes of a liar. But it didn't take long for Meagan to convince Baxter and Lefferts that his plans would pan out, that they all could get rich, if they gave it some time.

By nature Baxter was not a patient man. The trait had gotten him into as much trouble as it had gotten him out of. Impatience had prompted him to leave a complacent gang before a posse arrived thus saving his neck. It had also gotten him shot in the leg once for entering a bank too early.

Impatience gnawed at him again as he sat his horse by the stream that divided Meagan's land from Bedders' portion of the valley. The animal leisurely lapped up the water. Baxter's eyes were glazed with boredom when suddenly they cleared and he sat up. He thought he had seen Bedders in the valley tending his herd, but the man was nowhere in view. He had disappeared.

The temptation was too much for Baxter. He hitched his horse forward across the stream and trotted around Apple Rock. Carefully scanning the back valley, he could see that Bedders wasn't there either. For half an hour he herded small bunches of Bedders' cows back across the stream and spread them through the Meagan herd. Laziness and boredom overtook him soon, though. He grew tired of the job. What he really wanted was for Bedders to come charging out of nowhere and start shooting.

Some of the cattle were bunched across a narrow creek deep in the valley corner. Baxter decided to take these last few and call it a day. Splashing into the creek he noticed several cows scamper behind a hill. Following, Baxter saw with some surprise the gorge into which Bedders had gone. Baxter's eyes darkened with cruelty and a small smile grew underneath his matted beard as he urged his horse forward into the gorge.

CHAPTER SIX

Stretching below Bedders lay a valley nearly as big as his own flowing with high green grass. The sides were steep, carved mostly of limestone, and coloured with the occasional red drippings from an iron ore deposit or by scrub brush still green from summer. There were several clusters of trees here and there, and a narrow stream that came out through the rocks that may have originated behind his cabin. Dotted about the grass were cattle quietly grazing.

Bedders spurred the piebald forward into a gallop and began a fast circuit of the valley. Although some miles away, he was able to see the hills rising all around in an oval, enclosing the valley like a giant pen. He was desperate to confirm this, to find no way out other than the gorge, for that would mean no one else was using this land. Several times he stopped to examine folds in the hills, and each time he found a dead end. He located several caves, some of them with old Indian sign deep within their cool musty interiors. But none of the caves had been used recently.

The cattle had the scars of old brands, nothing recognizable. He counted as he circled the range and found nearly fifty head. Some of them were his, but the majority belonged to others from several seasons past. They were his now. And so was this valley. With it he had nearly twice the range and a real chance to survive the winter. Instantly he decided he would move the herd up here for the rest of the fall to allow the grass in the main valley to regenerate. Come winter he would take the herd down until he could determine how much damage winter did to this new range.

Several of his cows were coming up the trail through the gorge at a lope, smelling fresh grass. They crested the hill then jogged down into the open grass. Bedders pushed them along for a while then stopped to look in another cave. This one had a wide mouth with a low over-hang. It did not go very deep but it had several large flat rocks inside and what looked like an ancient firepit that had not been used in many long years. It was a comfort-able place and Bedders decided to make it his home when on this range.

A chunk of rock spat up in front of him without warn-ing, clipping his hat and knocking it from his head. An instant later came the echoing report of a rifle.

The piebald, standing at the cave mouth, screamed and stamped its feet but did not run. Bedders dived for the saddle and yanked the Remington from the scabbard. Two more shots pinged off the the sides of the cave, sending heavy bullets ricocheting. Bedders fell to the cave floor and rolled behind a concealing rock, levering off two quick, aimless shots. He hadn't seen the muzzle flash and with the ricochets had no idea where the shooter was hiding.

Outside the cave were more rocks and some deep verti-cal cracks that were carved into the steep hillside. He couldn't stay here waiting to get picked off, especially if there was more than one shooter. He needed some manoeuvring room.

Standing, he fired two rapid shots then slapped at the piebald's rear end as he flattened himself against the cave wall. He quickly slid forward to the mouth of the cave then squeezed himself into a crack in the valley wall that barely shielded him from view. It had taken a heartbeat but the movement had confused the shooter just long enough.

For a split second, in eerie silence, the thin limestone that Bedders hid behind began to splatter rock chips that bit into his face. Then he heard the sharp report of four echoing gunshots, melded together as if they were one. This hiding place, he decided, wasn't much better than the cave.

Bedders looked up and saw that there were handholds in the craggy rock. About twenty feet up, the crack angled back away from him, disappearing from view. He hoped it would offer a means of escape. Slowly working the lever of his rifle, Bedders ejected and caught the remaining shells and pocketed them. Then he tore off a piece of his shirt-sleeve and tied one end of it to the metal saddle ring soldered to the rifle's receiver and the other end to an unused belt loop on his pants. The rifle dangled awkwardly but at least he could carry it with him without fear of dropping it.

He climbed. When he reached the angle he found that this was shielded, too. He rested on a bench for a few minutes lying awkwardly on one shoulder while he untied his rifle and reloaded.

The shooter was far away, that much was certain. The delay between the bullet striking and the sound of the gun firing told him that. But if the shooter were within rifle range Bedders would be able to hit him, if he could find the man.

The bench inclined back among some rocks and

widened. Bedders crawled on his side, wary of the shooter below until he was able to slip behind a line of rounded boulders. Again he paused and this time dared look down into the valley. The piebald had run off a few hundred feet and was now champing at his bit. The mouth of the valley appeared to be open. There were several stunted trees growing where the hill crested just before the gorge opened like a river delta and spilled down into the valley. The head of a horse peaked out of the gorge, tossing about anxiously. It wanted to get down into the soft grass but something held it there.

Then Bedders saw a blue shirt. Just a piece of it but that was enough. It was off to the side of the gorge mouth, away from the scrawny trees and behind a clump of tall juniper bushes.

Bedders sighted his rifle and waited. The valley was the worst place for an ambush. If the shooter had waited until Bedders returned through the gorge he could have killed him easily. But out in the open valley there was no place for either man to hide well.

Impatience finally did the man in. He shifted his position, showing more of his blue shirt, barely discernible behind the blue-green of the juniper. Then he lifted his head, risking a quick scan of the hillside.

Bedders squeezed the trigger. Echoing, the shot fired several times on those valley walls. The man's hat went flying and a blue shirt fell out from behind the bushes. Bedders watched the man rise up on an elbow and pull his rifle around, taking a wavering bead on the muzzle flash he had seen. His aim already set, Bedders squeezed off another shot. The man jerked back and flopped into the grass.

Bedders waited twenty minutes watching for movement before climbing back down to the valley floor. Scraped, and bleeding from a dozen tiny cuts, he retrieved the piebald and walked the animal toward the dead man.

It was Lloyd Baxter. He had two large holes in his torso.

Looking at the man Bedders began to shake and hatred swelled in him. He wanted to kill the man again, his rage was so great. He let the fury take him, not wanting to think about why Baxter would ambush him, or on whose orders. Baxter was a thug. He had known that the first day he met the man. He knew then that his dream for a quiet piece of land to call his own might crumble, that he would have to fight. But whom would he fight? Certainly not Baxter alone. The man was mean, but not intelligent. He was a like a mongrel needing always to be on a leash. His saddle partner, Lefferts, was smarter, but he was no leash holder. Lefferts was lazy. Bedders had seen all summer how he got Baxter to do the heavy work.

Bedders stopped his musing before it developed further. He did not want to think about the terrible betrayal that awaited him in those thoughts.

Numbly he went about catching up Baxter's grey horse and stripping it. With a slap he sent the animal running deep into the valley. The saddle and blanket he put in the cave, along with Baxter's gunbelt and pistol and long rifle. Then he dragged the body to a soft patch of dirt behind a rock and, digging a shallow grave, rolled Baxter into it. He covered the body, hat and all, and left no marker save the blank stone.

Although he had moved mechanically, his heart heavy and his thoughts jumbled, his mind was lucid enough to reach a decision. He would not to tell Meagan about the incident. Their friendship was already strained. Bedders did not want to test it further. And if he were to fight he would need every advantage he could get.

*

Bedders sat atop the piebald, the scratchy tips of a willow brushing against his cheek as he waited beneath the tree and looked down into the hollow below. The sun still had strength, even this late into fall, and Bedders was grateful for the temporary shade. There was just a touch of brisk-ness in the air, though, and a change in smell brought about by dying grass and turning leaves that foretold of the winter to come. This would be one of the last bright, warm days of the year and much of the town of Lander had gathered in the hollow below for a harvest celebra-tion.

On the back side of the hill Meagan had paused to greet his ranch hand, the small and cheerful Lefferts. The man had ridden up at a gallop, dust cloud in his wake, hat bent to the wind. Meagan rode out a little to meet him, but not far enough away that Bedders couldn't hear what was said, their voices drifting up to him on a warm breeze.

'Hell if I know where he is,' said Lefferts with a shrug. His cheerful face was slightly creased with worry lines.

'Did you check . . . everywhere?' Meagan's back tingled thinking Bedders was watching him. He turned quickly to see his friend at the crest of the shallow hill looking away.

'All of them.' Lefferts spoke tightly.

Meagan sat atop his black, shiny horse and thought a moment. 'It doesn't make sense. He say anything about leaving?'

'No. We was pards. He had no place special to go, and no one to see.'

A sudden thought came to Meagan. 'Check in town. And then ask . . . the other. Understand?'

'Sure,' Lefferts said, nodding. He reined his horse with

a violent tug and kicked it into a gallop.

Meagan sat for a moment, thinking. Then he turned and trotted up the hill to Bedders.

'Heh! You can't keep good ranch hands I guess,' he said. Bedders was surprised just how easily and naturally Meagan's good humour came after disturbing news. Had he seen such behaviour in his friend when they were younger? Or was this something new? Something recently learned?

'He'll turn up,' Bedders said blandly and instantly realized he should have said nothing.

'You haven't seen him, friend? Have you?' There was a hint of suspicion in Meagan's voice. More than that, there was curiosity, as if he were looking at Bedders differently now.

'No.'

With a kick, Bedders sent the piebald down into the hollow. Meagan had insisted they come together. They had seen so little of each other during the past year he wanted to spend time with his friend. For his part Bedders hadn't been certain he would go to the harvest celebration. Everyone was invited, but he felt awkwardness crawl up his spine when he thought about going. Meagan would be there, he knew, because Emily would attend. Bedders did not like the thought of watching the two of them together. But Meagan had insisted in a forceful but light-hearted way. It was so strange for Bedders to see danger behind Meagan's friendly face. But there was no mistaking it.

The hollow, spotted with bur oak and box elder and a large horse chestnut, all bearing bright colours of the season, was filled with Lander townsfolk. A string of buckboards formed a boundary to the gathering. Someone had erected a corral by stretching rope around a few closely spaced aspen. Kids were running about picking the last of the chokecherries. Tables had been set up randomly and women were busily covering them with cloths and plates of bread and fruit. At the back of one wagon someone had brought a tub of beer and a few of the young boys were buzzing around it. A dozen men had just started digging three pits, into which raw native coal and wood would go to start cooking fires. The day was early yet, and the festivities would go long into the night.

Bedders looked but did not see Emily.

Side by side Bedders and Meagan rode down into the hollow, angling around the gathering toward the rope corral. They both noticed how the men stopped their work and turned to follow them with unfriendly eyes. They said nothing, just stared hotly. The women paused, too, and gathered to whisper.

'Looks like a fun party,' Meagan said. He smiled lightly, but his voice was a little tight.

'Maybe we should go.'

'I ain't never run from nothing in my life, Nix,' said Meagan, coldly. 'I won't start now.'

But Bedders wanted to run. He was afraid. Not of the men, some of whom flexed their fists, all but inviting a fight. And not of the cruel whispers of the women. His fear was borne of a certainty of what Meagan would do once drink flowed and the conspiring of men became obvious and he grew bolder with irrational hatred. For Meagan had come wearing his gun, and he pat it comfortingly as he stepped from the corral into the centre of the party.

For a moment the two men stood alone as everyone turned back to their chores. Meagan smiled, looking at some of the younger women setting tables.

'Got me some work to do, Nix,' he said, saluting cavalierly, then sauntering away.

Bedders wandered toward the pits.

'There you are,' Amos Cavanaugh called. The man was stripped to the waist with beads of sweat streaming down his smooth chest. He had a pickaxe in one hand and a shovel in another. 'Which'll it be?'

Bedders sighed heavily, relief washing over him. He called for the pickaxe and caught it by the worn hickory handle as Cavanaugh tossed it to him. Then he stripped to the waist, too, shouldered into the group of men, still surly and suspicious, and began swinging the axe. He felt knots in his back begin to dissolve as he attacked the hard dirt. For some reason it gave him a deep satisfaction to pummel the ground this way, and they all worked in silence for long minutes.

Some time later, as Bedders took a breather and the shovellers moved in to clear the broken earth, Cavanaugh asked, 'How're the new steers doing?'

'They're all right. If I can just keep 'em through winter.' Bedders took a tin cup from a pail and splashed some water over his heated face before swallowing a mouthful.

'I'm glad. Mr Bedders and his friend divided the valley,' Cavanaugh told the gathered men. 'They're each working half of it on their own.'

This brought a rumble of quiet talk from the men.

'Hell, that valley ain't big enough to divide, boy,' a plump man that Bedders knew as Jeggins said. 'Not for a man who's looking to build an empire.'

'I don't need much, sir. It's big enough for my plans.'

'Not fer yer friend,' someone grumbled.

'You dividing at the crik?' asked another.

'That's right. I've got the inside piece.'

'You gave your friend the better half,' Jeggins said and a few of them laughed good-naturedly.

Bedders smiled shyly. 'I guess that's right, too.'

They turned back to their work, now shoulder to shoulder, and slowly developed a rhythm. The pits were dug quickly and filled with coal and wood and lit to a roaring blaze. They congratulated themselves, shaking hands and slapping sweaty backs. Bedders found himself in the middle of it, smiling, a lump in his throat.

'I heard you took on that ornery Christopher fella a ways back,' Jeggins said. 'No offense, Amos, but that fella was trouble.'

'I know it, Bill. That's why I fired his sorry backside.'

'Now if you'd just take on that Lincoln fella . . .' someone suggested.

Smiling, Amos said, 'Hey, there. Lincoln's got his uses.'

'Yeah. If'n we ever run outa mountains!'

'How about it, Bedders,' Jeggins asked, 'you planning on taking him on?'

Bedders demurred a bit then said, 'I'll wait 'til I grow up some for that.'

The gathering laughed. A few hands reached in and tousled Bedders' red curls, a few more slapped him on the back, almost knocking him to the ground. Out of the corner of his eye he saw Meagan sitting at a table, a straw sticking out of his mouth and a cold look in his eyes.

Cavanaugh nodded to Bedders and the two men walked to a table with bowls of apples and plates of cornbread. Cavanaugh took an apple and bit into it, nearly obliterating the thing.

'Butchered a steer they'll be roasting soon. Them fire pits belong to Jeggins now. Hampress butchered a sow and we got chickens from half a dozen farms.' Already Jeggins was working the meat on to spits that would be lifted up over the fire.

'Quite a turnout.'

'You'll meet most of them before it ends. They're your neighbours.'

Bedders nodded.

Champing into another apple Cavanaugh said, 'Your friend seems at home.'

Meagan was still seated at the table. He was pilfering from a basket of chokecherries as he scanned the activity.

'I suppose so.'

'Some of the men think he's a might too at home. Men like Danelles.'

For a split second anger flared in Bedders. Then he looked into Cavanaugh's eyes and saw only concern.

'There was a time in this part of the country blood flowed like rivers. 'Tween the Indians and rustlers and men trying to carve out empires there was a lot of lead thrown. Now I won't deny my part in it. I fought for my land. But I've paid for it, too. Lost a wife and a son. I've got a daughter coming to age soon and I'm grateful to still have her. I've lost good men, too. The land I take now I buy, or get in a grant from the government. It's enough for me.'

Bedders watched the man closely as he talked. Cavanaugh had gotten wistful and spoke softly. For a long moment he was silent.

'But it's not enough for some, is it?'

Bedders shrugged. 'Don't know as I'd know what to do with as much land as you've got, Mr Cavanaugh,' he said.

'Your friend would.'

That hung between them for a few minutes. Bedders couldn't look at the man now. He was right, of course.

Meagan wanted more. That he was starting to crowd Danelles' range was proof of that.

'Folks around here remember what it was like twenty years ago. They don't want it again. You understand that, don't you?'

'Yes.' Again, Bedders looked over at his friend sitting casually at a rustic table, chatting with a shy girl or making faces at some of the children. He seemed to radiate a dangerous charm that attracted the innocent. 'He's a friend,' Bedders said, but his words sounded hollow, unconvincing. 'I can talk to him.'

Strangely, he found his feet heavy as he turned from Cavanaugh and watched his friend idling on a narrow bench, seemingly oblivious to the hostility around him. Yet Bedders knew Meagan had keen senses, especially about people. He would not have missed feeling the anger directed toward him upon his arrival, nor the suspicion and fear that lingered in the air around some of the women. Talking to him here would be useless, perhaps even dangerous. Bedders would have to wait for a better time.

An hour later Emily and her father arrived. The girl drove the family buckboard and her father was perched atop the bench holding on to two leather straps that had been looped and nailed to the seat to steady him. Several men rushed forward, including Meagan, who deftly removed John Patterson's wheelchair, setting it beside the buckboard. Emily gently smiled at him.

Other men helped Patterson down and, with grunts and a curse or two, settled the big man into the chair.

'Must be your daughter's good cookin'!' one of the helpers exclaimed jovially. 'You've been puttin' on weight!' All the men smiled warmly at Patterson, who sincerely returned their pleasantries. Standing back from them, though, Bedders could see a twinge of guilt in his eyes, maybe shame. The man struggled to maintain his dignity.

Meagan stepped behind the wheelchair, taking hold of the bare wood handles, and started to push Patterson toward the gathering. Emily stopped him and took the handles herself, smiling a little as she nudged Meagan away.

'Bedders, my boy. It is good to see you.'

Bedders had come forward like many of the townspeople to greet the man.

'Hello, Emily. Mr Patterson.'

'Son, call me John.'

'We haven't seen you since your return, Mr Bedders' – was her voice a little chilly? – 'you promised to come by for dinner.'

Patterson reached back to take his daughter's hand. It was a simple gesture, and he said nothing, but Bedders saw that her stiffened back relaxed, just a little.

'I've wanted to come around, but my being so far from town, I would never know when you're away on a picnic,' Bedders said, hating himself the moment he uttered the words.

'The man's busy with his ranch,' Patterson interjected. 'I understand you got some new cattle. Good luck with them. Come sit with me later and jaw a while over a beer.'

'I will, sir.' Bedders spoke numbly, his mind elsewhere. He had just realized Emily wore a leather vest that was different from the one he had last seen her wearing. There was something familiar about it, although for a moment he couldn't place it. And then it hit him. He recognized the colouring of it from one of his cows that

91

had died last winter. Brown with white spots, which was common enough. But this animal had had a small reddish blotch at the edge of one of its white spots. The vest had the same reddish colouring.

Bedders looked up to see Emily watching him. She raised a rather haughty eyebrow then pushed her father toward some of the other men.

'Well, Nix,' Meagan said, grinning ear to ear, 'looks like the field is clear now!' Walking away, laughing, he slapped Bedders on the back.

The celebration progressed. Food was served and eaten. Beer flowed and someone had brought a jug of home brew that found its way through the hollow despite being chased after by a committee of intolerant women. Soon after, as lanterns and torches were lit, a fiddler stumbled his way to the top of a table, getting his dirty feet slapped for walking on the tablecloth. He scratched out a few tunes with folks singing and joining in.

Throughout the day Bedders had watched Emily as she moved about the party, tending to her father, talking with the women, and playing with the children. A cloud of young men tried to follow her. She was courteous and sweet with each when cornered for a moment, but never lingered for very long with any of them. Even Meagan had had difficulty corralling some time with her. Bedders had not tried to compete. But when the fiddler changed to dance music he stepped forward.

'Miss Patterson, would you care to dance?' he asked, his back so stiff he thought it would crack. Other young men had come forward, too.

Meagan was instantly at his side. 'Now, I remember a fine day not so long ago,' he said to Emily, 'at our picnic when you promised me every dance at the celebration.'

Meagan had crowded Bedders, using his shoulder to muscle in front of the others.

Emily laughed, just the slightest strain showing in her voice. She looked at the two friends, and the two or three other expectant young men and a terrible thrill ran through her. 'I truly don't recall that, Mr Meagan.'

'Oh, the entire day is imprinted deeply in my memory. I am just certain that is what you said. I wouldn't lie about a thing like that.'

'Of course not.' Her face was getting tense now, enough so that Bedders saw it and thought about withdrawing. Damn it, no! He wanted to dance with the girl. She saw something in his face at that moment and calmed. 'But it wouldn't be fair to these gentlemen not to dance with them at least once.'

'I don't care about fair.'

'Emily,' Bedders said, leaning forward, 'I believe I. . . .'

'Andrew! There you are!' Ignoring Bedders and Meagan, Emily reached out for a tall, skinny blond boy who stood back of the others, hands folded, shy. 'I believe we were going to dance.'

Before Meagan could say another word, Emily had stepped into Andrew's surprised arms and twirled away to the music.

'You jes' wanna take everythin', don'tcha boy?'

Meagan spun around, his hand darting to the pistol at his side. Gone was the mask of casual affability. His eyes glared hate.

'Pistol' Nate Danelles wore no gun and neither did the six angry men standing beside him. Danelles held a whiskey bottle by the neck like a club. They had all been drinking, the smell of alcohol was thick around them.

Danelles was a short man, maybe five foot eight, but he

had a barrel chest and thick, powerful legs that arched just a little from too much time in the saddle. He seemed rooted deep as he stood facing Meagan, like the large horse chestnut tree in the centre of the hollow.

'What I can take,' Meagan said, tauntingly, 'I will.'

'Let's go, Abel.' Bedders put a hand to Meagan's arm and was violently shaken loose. Bedders turned away.

'I'm staying,' Meagan said.

'The hell ya will,' Danelles yelled. ''Least ways not on my range.'

'That's free range, Pistol Nate. I checked. Learned that trick from my buddy Nix. You don't own the land and I aim to graze where I can.'

Two of the men started to move around Danelles but the rancher stopped them.

'I've fought bigger'n you, pup. And if ya wanna see why's they give me that nickname, why jes' keep a-pushin'.'

The smile on Meagan's face was cold and hateful. 'OK.'

Bedders came back leading their horses. He let the black nuzzle Meagan's back to get his attention, then said. 'Let's ride.'

For a long minute Bedders thought his friend would refuse. Then Meagan climbed aboard the black and spurred the animal into a gallop. Bedders followed without a backward glance.

When he caught up, Meagan said, 'Why, Nix, I didn't get my dance.'

'I think you've danced enough for one night.'

The next day it rained, adding to the gloom Bedders felt. It ate at him deeply, paining his heart and his gut. His jaw hurt, too, and found that he had been clenching it. He had been sitting in his cabin, rain drizzling on the roof, staring into the fire blazing in the stone hearth, lamenting what had been lost last night at the harvest celebration, when a knock came to the door. He hadn't heard anyone approach. He sat, unmoving. The door opened after a moment and Emily walked in.

She said nothing but simply stood in the doorframe, rain patting the stone walk behind her. Her arms were wrapped around a small bundle covered in a towel. He turned to look at her, her appearance stern and dark against the misty grey backdrop. She moved into the cabin and set the bundle on the table, uncovering it and revealing a basket filled with food.

She was wearing the new vest.

'I didn't think you'd eaten much last night,' she told him, unpacking the basket. She shrugged looking down at the table. There was enough food for three men, a feast that included a whole apple pie. 'The men drank the beer,' she said apologetically.

'I don't need the beer.'

He stood up on wobbly legs and went to the table. She wouldn't look up at him. He stood very close to her, his heart racing uncertainly, then reached out to take her hand. For a moment he thought she would pull away, her hand had tensed with a jerk. But she let him take it then let herself be pulled gently to him. She couldn't help but look at him when lightly he pushed her chin up toward his face.

'Emily. . . .'

'I'm sorry we missed that dance,' she said quickly, her voice almost a whisper.

'I wanted to dance,' he told her.

The pounding of horses' hoofs suddenly thundered outside the cabin. Bedders was just turning toward the gun hanging on a nail by the door when Meagan burst into the room. A cold half-smile was chiselled on to the man's face in a vain attempt to hide the seething hatred that radiated off of him.

'What a fool I was telling you not to go to town too often,' Meagan said. 'And here the town is coming to you. That's a lovely picnic basket, Miss Patterson, almost as lovely as the one we shared.'

'I have to go.' Emily took the towel and, turning, folded it to keep her nervous hands busy. Meagan stepped in front of her.

'I'm sure you just got here. Stay.'

She was stern again, and angry. 'I have to go.' At the door she stopped to look back at Bedders. 'You'll come to dinner sometime soon.'

After she had gone, Meagan laughed and sat down at the table. He pawed through the food, snatching a bit of steak and taking a bite.

'Lefferts. Get in here.'

Casting a lewd glance toward the departing Emily, Lefferts sidled into the room.

'Good grub.'

Swallowing his disappointment, Bedders said, 'Take what you want.'

'Oh, I will, Nix. I will.'

Lefferts joined Meagan at the table and began devouring the food. Bedders took a piece of fried chicken and retreated to a stump chair by the fire. But he wasn't hungry.

'Didn't see much of your herd around, Nix.'

'They're around. They collect at the end of the valley sometimes.'

'Uh-huh. Say, you ain't seen Baxter around, have you?'

'You asked me that yesterday.'

Grinning, Meagan said, 'Why, so I did.'

Bedders took a deep breath, steeling himself. 'Abel, you got quite a herd there. You've never raised cattle so maybe you don't see that you've got too many for your end of the valley.'

'I reckon you're right, pard,' he said, grinning. 'That is if I planned to keep to my end of the valley.'

'You'll get a fight from Danelles if you push too much further with him.'

Meagan shrugged. 'OK.'

Stunned, Bedders asked, 'Do you really want bloodshed, Abel?'

'There doesn't have to be. I'll be on free range. Told Danelles that last night. If a fight's coming, he'll start it. And I'll finish it.'

'Look, Abel, let's take our herd and ride out of here,' Bedders said, coming to the table. 'We'll find better land, a place that doesn't flood so much in winter. A bigger place for us to stretch out on.'

Meagan laughed. 'I knew it! I just knew it! Well, you go on, Nix. I'll be glad to have the whole valley.'

'What are you talking about?'

'You're a wanderer, Nix. I've known you since we both started walking. You've never been one to sit still. You lit out when you was fourteen on that giant black mare and you never did look back.'

'I came back for you, didn't I?'

'Sure you did. You wanted someone to side you on the trail. That's fine. I wanted out of that two-bit town, too. You gave me the courage to do it. But you won't stay put, Nix. You'll roam, and soon. You've never put in a full day's work, seven days a week in your whole life. You can't keep it up much longer. And when you decide to roam, I'll buy your 'stead and your stock. I'll have this valley. I mean to have it all. It's good land and there is money to be made here.' There was a fire in the man. As he talked he leaned forward, rising up, yearning. It was like that first day when Bedders had shown him the valley. Meagan had been a coiled spring, a man hungry and full of hate for the things he had never had, the things that had passed him by.

'Sounds almost like you want to take it from me.'

'I won't have to, Nix. You'll sell it and you'll ride on because that's what you do. I'll have it all, then. All of it.'

A chill ran through Bedders. He looked out the door past the falling, misty rain and the muddy grass to where Emily's horse had stood. He pictured her in Meagan's arms, smiling, and something dark began to grow within him.

CHAPTER SEVEN

Snow covered the spiny north ridge that enclosed
Bedders' hidden valley, the wind whipping curls of snow-
dust off it, spraying the icy flakes like glitter down the
steep, rocky hillside. Patches of snow had piled up at the
base of the south slope, too, but the valley floor was rela-
tively clear. The icy wind that howled above only occasionally stabbed down into the valley. It was cold, to be sure,
but protected from the elements. Bedders' herd had fared
well through the fall and the worst parts of the winter.

Bedders had lost only three head so far, and none of
them to cold or lack of graze. In fact, the hidden valley had
done remarkably well in supporting his three hundred
head. There were patches down to the nubbins, but most of
the short-cropped grass would come back strong this spring.

Bundled in a woollen scarf and long coat, hat pulled
down to his ears, Bedders rode a slow circuit around the
valley. No one had discovered the entrance to it yet, nor
had they questioned Bedders' long absences from his
range. Meagan especially had not seemed to notice,
himself rarely at home. Bedders had gone back to his
cabin several times, rarely finding Meagan's cows on his
side of the range. He wondered if that was a line Meagan
didn't want to cross. That he might crowd Danelles but

not his friend. If that was so, then perhaps there was some hope for the man, Bedders thought.

He had run into Lefferts once, who had come out for a ride on an unseasonably warm fall day. The ranch hand casually asked after Bedders' herd. Lefferts had not ventured farther than Apple Rock, though, so Bedders told him the cattle were deeper in the valley where the grass was taller. If Lefferts suspected a lie, it didn't show. The man didn't really care. He was on his way to town and when he returned that night it was too dark and he was too drunk to see much anyway.

The secret had been kept and Bedders was grateful for a second chance to start his own outfit. He had spoken to Cavanaugh on the drive last spring about the cattle market. The rancher said he would fold into his herd how ever many cows Bedders wanted to sell and drive them to market come next fall. By then, with calving, he might have three hundred and fifty or more fat beeves. Selling a couple hundred of them would give Bedders a good stake for the coming years.

Despite the chill air he felt a warm glow of satisfaction.

Finishing his circuit, Bedders returned to the cave in which he had made his temporary home. He had built a façade at the front of the chamber, with a shuttered window and a door big enough to admit the piebald if need be. He had erected a canvas roof in the short gap between the log wall and the cave's rock face to keep out the weather. Inside he had built a stone stove against the crevasse that he had once used to escape Baxter's ambush. The crevasse acted as a chimney. It was quite warm inside.

Bedders had just pulled the saddle from the piebald when he saw a rider tentatively enter the valley. The rider paused as Bedders had done the first time and sat in awe.

Slipping into the cave through the door, Bedders grabbed his Remington and waited.

Bundled against the cold as the rider was, it took some time before Bedders recognized Emily. He stepped out to greet her.

For long moments she didn't say anything. Bedders saw the shock on her face and helped her down from the horse and into the warmed cave. She huffed a quiet laugh seeing the homey touches inside: tick bedding, lanterns, cookstove, and a rude table erected on top of a flat rock.

'Your winter home, Mr Bedders?' she asked, finally.

He smiled. 'I guess that's right. How did you find me?'

'I came out to get you for dinner. You do remember your promise I expect.'

'I remember. I've just. . . .'

'You've just been busy. Too busy to eat it appears.' For a second just the barest edge came into her voice, then fled as her smile widened. 'Yet not too busy to carve out a warm camp.'

Bedders ducked his head, embarrassed. 'Emily, this is very important to me.'

She came to him, pulling off her hat and setting free her long, warm hair. She stood very close and looked up at him, deep into him. 'I understand. I'm glad it's important to you.'

'How did you find me?' he asked again, breaking a long silence between them.

'You weren't at the cabin so I rode deeper into the valley thinking you might be there. I hadn't seen you in town. I noticed how few cows you had and. . . .' Her voice trailed off and she turned away from him.

'You thought I had pulled out?'

'Or got rustled.' There was a hint of defiance in her

voice. She hadn't liked the smirking grin that had come to his face. 'Then I saw a couple of cows disappear behind a rock and followed them.'

He smiled. 'How's the pass?'

'A foot or more of snow all through it.'

Bedders nodded. 'I think it's time for me to bring the herd back. They've about played out this range and I guess the other valley has grass enough for the rest of the winter.'

'Not so fast!' She had thrown hands to her hips and jut out her jaw. 'You promised to come to dinner, and that's just what you'll do, Mr . . . oh, do you really want me to keep calling you Mr Bedders?'

'I guess not.' He thought his face might break from the size of the smile he was wearing.

'Well, then, I can't call you Carrot, and I won't call you Nix. Your mother must have given you a proper name.'

'She did, but it never stuck.'

Emily cocked an impatient eyebrow and tilted her head.

'It's Morton.' She was not any good at hiding her amusement. 'Not a rough and rowdy kinda name, is it?'

'No it isn't, Morton. But I like it just the same.'

Bedders went out and saddled the piebald then rode with Emily into the pass. On the other side, Bedders entered the valley first, looking around for anyone who might have seen him. The range was empty. Emily joined him then and they rode at a trot toward the pass to Lander. As they passed Apple Rock Bedders saw two riders working their way through Meagan's herd. Neither Lefferts nor Meagan were in sight.

'Wait here,' he told Emily as he spurred his horse into a gallop toward the strangers.

Hearing his approach, they turned to meet him.

'Howdy,' Bedders said, tersely.

'Howdy.'

Bedders had glanced at the horses' flanks and had seen Nate Danelles' Double Bar R brand on each.

'You boys lost?' Bedders didn't recognize either man. One was slightly taller than the other was, one was blond and the other black-haired. Other than that they looked cut from the same sturdy bolt of cloth.

'Headin' on through to Cavanaugh's place. Gonna be jawin' with him,' said the blond.

'Uh-huh. And I suppose you were in town this morning when you decided that.'

'That's exactly right. So we took the pass. Didn't think you'd mind.'

'No. Happy to be neighbourly.'

They had held their horses very still, and none of them had strayed a hand toward their guns. Since the harvest celebration Bedders had taken to wearing his constantly. He saw that the two riders were likewise armed.

'Meagan's cows more interesting than Mr Danelles'?'

'How's that?' The black-haired fellow had tensed just a little.

'Well, you boys were working your way through the herd like you were looking for something.'

'Not really. We lost some head recently, thought they mighta got mixed up in this bunch.'

'Are they here?'

'No.'

The black-haired man snarled a bit. 'Might clumsy with the branding iron, though. Sloppy, I'd say.'

'Take it up with Meagan. These animals belong to him.'

'Do they?'

Bedders took a long, slow breath. 'You got something to say, mister, then say it.'

'He's sloppy with his iron, is all. Hard to tell just what brand some of these are.'

No one moved for several long seconds. The blond seemed nervous now. He shot several taut glances at his partner as he absent-mindedly bit his lower lip.

'I think you both best be on your way.'

Without another word the two men reined their horses around and rode off at a trot.

'Is everything OK?' Emily asked as he returned.

Bedders smiled and said, 'I'm hungry. Let's go to dinner.'

A short time later, looking at the Patterson's brimming dining table, Bedders realized Emily had gotten up quite early to prepare the meal and yet leave enough time to ride out and bring him back to eat it. She was certainly a determined young woman. Bedders found he liked that of her. She wasn't a wallflower, or some dainty thing to be protected and taken care of. She'd do her share of taking care, when it came time. She would be a partner, someone with whom he could share a life.

John Patterson looked well and he ate even better. It was easy to see how the man had attained his bulk. Emily's cooking was finer than anything Bedders had ever tasted. He found himself matching Patterson fork for fork right up until Emily brought out two mooseapple pies. Patterson didn't even bother to dish out any on to his plate. He simply stuck a fork into one of them and began eating. Bedders laughed, realizing he had been beaten, then cut two hunks from the second pie, for him and Emily. Coffee came to the table in two pots, one of these being set at Patterson's elbow.

'The only vice I've left, Morton,' Patterson said. 'Eating.'

'You do it well, sir.'

'Hell, I do it exceedingly well!'

During the meal Emily had revealed Bedders' true first name and Patterson had taken to it immediately. Emily had also tried to signal Bedders that he should mention the hidden valley. He had been reluctant at first but finally told Patterson about it in detail. Now over coffee the older man gave the subject some thought.

'Don't think anyone's ever mentioned it. I can tell you it's not on any of the maps. Of course, that don't mean much. The army wasn't that thorough in their scouting back in the sixties. Too busy chasing the Cheyenne and the Arapaho and even the Sioux. Wild times, it was. Lucky to've kept my hair, I can tell you that.'

'I can graze it, then?'

'Don't see why not. None of the folks in this country would touch it, locked in as it is. 'Course, it would be better for you if you had full control over the main valley.'

'Half of it belongs to Meagan.'

'I know, son. But you've got to know he can't last. Folks don't like him. And he's done a bit to help that along.' Bedders looked up sharply. 'I think you know what I mean.'

The jovial mood of the meal had vanished under a pall. Bedders turned moody. 'I don't know that. Not for certain.'

'No one does. He's been careful. But his herd is three times what it was when he first came here. And that's just what folks can see.'

'I guess folks talk a lot in this town.'

Patterson stiffened but kept his voice pleasant. 'Folks in any town talk. Meagan's giving them plenty to jaw on.'

'Dad, please.'

'He needs to hear this, Emily. Morton, you've got friends in this country. They've all seen you're not part of whatever Meagan is doing. Cavanaugh has helped you. He wouldn't do that unless he thought you were worth it. I want to help you, too, but all I can offer is advice.' Bedders had turned away from the table, sullen. Now he looked back to Patterson. 'You need to make a decision soon about your friend. The way he's going something bad will happen. You've been insulated in that valley of yours. You haven't seen what's happening. Or maybe you haven't wanted to see it. But it's right there in front of you now.'

'Say the word, Mr Patterson,' Bedders said, almost defiantly. 'Tell me what he's doing.'

'You know it, Morton. He's rustling. And from people who won't stand for it.'

'That's enough, Dad.'

Emily got up from the table, dropping a dishcloth she had wrung into knots. She pulled Bedders to his feet and brought him out to the front room and sat him by the fire.

'It's not as bad as all of that, Emily. He's my friend. I can help him.'

'Can you?'

Bedders looked into her fiery eyes and saw that she thought Meagan was beyond help. She was worried. Funny, he thought, how he could tell that by just looking at her. How many times had they met? How many times had they talked in the past two years? Perhaps a dozen. Yet he was reading her thoughts, as she must have been reading his. She was worried for him.

'I want to help him,' he told her.

'Then do it, if he'll let you. And if he won't. . . .'

Bedders nodded.

They talked for a few minutes about nothing at all. Bedders kept avoiding her eyes. He told himself that he was foolish to feel shame for what Meagan was doing. But he didn't want her to see the shame he felt; he didn't want to lose her love. For she did love him, he could see that now, and was unsure he was deserving of those powerful emotions.

He left after that, thanking the Pattersons for their hospitality. For a while, he wandered through the town lost in thought, mindless of the cold and the glare of the bald, setting sun. When his shivering became overpowering he sought out the dry goods store with the sudden thought that he needed to replenish his larder.

'There you are!' Meagan appeared on the walk bundled in a heavy pelt coat, slapping his arms. 'Guess we had us the same thought.'

Bedders nodded, reaching for the door to the store.

'How about I buy you a drink, friend. That ride is a cold one and my bones need warming.'

They entered the Owl Creek saloon two doors down, grateful for the musty warmth. Two coal stoves burned redly, sending waves of heat out into the sparsely populated room. Several men sat in the back slowly working a few hands of poker. Two drovers occupied another table, a bottle of whiskey between them, their heads back against the wall, hats down over their eyes. The soft rattle of their snoring could be heard above the tinkle of chips being tossed.

Meagan ordered two whiskeys, dropping a shiny dollar on to the rough-hewn bar. They drank silently. Meagan ordered a second and downed that one, too, even as Bedders nursed his first glass.

'Feel like I could live in one of them stoves,' Meagan said, cheerfully. The bartender grunted and turned away. Meagan scowled then shrugged off the barman's rudeness.

'Ya might jes' have to get used to a place like that.'

Meagan turned toward the door slowly. Framed there

were the two riders Bedders had seen that morning – the blond and the black-haired man. Their hands rested anxiously on their gun butts.

Meagan smiled and let his arms stretch out to fall on to the bar. 'Well, I kinda like this place, fellas, long as I can warm myself on occasion.'

'You might find it healthier to move on,' the blond said.

'Might say the same about you two.'

Bedders put a hand on Meagan's arm. The gesture sparked a hateful look from his friend.

'That's enough, Abel. We've got chores to do.'

'Stay out'n this, Bedders,' the black-haired man said.

'Yes, friend, stay out.' Despite the easy smile on Meagan's face his voice was tense and mean.

'No. We're going, you two. Step aside.'

Bedders pulled Meagan away from the bar and pushed him toward the door. Meagan shuffled his feet as he neared the two Danelles riders, grinning tauntingly at them. With a shove, Bedders pushed his friend back out into the cold, down toward the dry goods store.

'Never figured you for a coward, Nix.'

'I'm not. I'm no fool, either. Those men wanted to kill you.'

Meagan laughed. 'Looked to me like they wanted to die.'

Bedders shoved Meagan into the store and held him against the door, a small bell jangling above their heads.

'Look here, Abel, things are getting out of hand. But they're not too far gone. We can still make things right.'

'I aim to, Nix. I'll make 'em right. Righter than they've ever been.'

Before he could stop himself, Bedders slapped his friend's face. 'Stop talking like that.'

Something changed in Meagan. No longer did he have the easy, careless grin he had worn for the past two years. Slowly, a grimace of hate overtook his face and his eyes became wild with anger.

'Righter than they've ever been,' he said, coldly. 'I've been living off'n other men so long and I don't aim to do it no more. Do you hear me? I've got something now and I'll hold on to it, even if it means killing a few stupid rannies. Now, let go of me, Nix. And don't ever lay hands on me again or I'll forget we're friends.' The smile came back for a second, but there was nothing but cruelty in it now.

Bedders released him and walked away.

'Here now, you two,' said the pale clerk, 'if you want to fight take it outside.'

'Aw, take it easy, toothpick. We come in to buy from you.'

Suddenly the door slammed open, the tiny bell above it jangling violently. The blond was standing there, hand hovering above his gun.

'We wasn't done with you, rustler,' the man said. Meagan turned and as he moved he unbuttoned his heavy coat. With a shrug it fell off his shoulders to the floor. He stepped around a dress mannequin, fingers flexing in anticipation.

'Well, I'm done with you.'

Bedders pulled at the store clerk, frozen with fear, dragging him out of the line of fire. It was too late now to stop it. Someone, Bedders knew, would die.

The sound of a boot heel scuffing on the floor alerted Bedders suddenly to movement. He whirled to see the blond man's partner creeping into the store through a back door. His pistol was drawn and aimed at Meagan's unsuspecting head.

'Drop it,' Bedders ordered.

The black-haired man spun and raised his gun, firing wildly. Something shattered behind Bedders' left ear. Bedders drew even as the shot's echo began dying and fired. The black-haired man corkscrewed around, grabbing at his shoulder. His gun fired again in the spasm of movement sending hot lead into a large can of peaches. Another shot blasted in the close room, followed instantly by the shattering of glass and the sound of boots running on the boardwalk.

Bedders looked around and saw Meagan still standing, laughing nervously.

'That blond fella lit out when you plugged his pardner,' Meagan said.

'See here,' the clerked squeaked. 'You have to go.'

Bedders ignored him. The black-haired man was lying on the floor, groaning. Bedders knelt beside him, taking the man's gun, and giving it to the clerk.

'Get a doctor to him right away,' he told the tremulous man. 'And get the marshal.'

'Ain't had a marshal for six months, but I'll get the doctor.' The clerk ran out of the store, grateful to get away with his skin.

'You had my back, pardner. Thank you.'

Bedders whirled on Meagan. Bile rose up in his throat as he wondered if he had done the right thing.

They were silent on the ride back to their valley. The cold helped to keep each man quiet and contained within his own thoughts. Bedders felt as if everything was slipping away from him, like it was all made of sand and running through his fingers. He looked at his friend's back, hunched inside the large coat, and experienced a new emotion. Resentment. The thought turned his stomach and he tried desperately to bury it deep within his heart.

CHAPTER EIGHT

They were waiting in the valley, six of them just across the ice-covered creek. Three of them were out among the cattle leaning over in their saddles, looking at the brands. Danelles was at the centre of his men facing the valley mouth across the creek, his compact body like a plug of chaw sitting inside a heavy brown coat. One of his riders motioned to him and Danelles reacted by turning his horse around. He carried a Winchester across his saddle, cocked and ready.

Bedders had seen them before Meagan, who was slumped forward in the saddle, huddled against the cold. For a moment he thought about turning toward his cabin and the warmth it promised, but he didn't like the look of that welcoming committee.

Now Meagan saw them and he sat bolt upright in the saddle. Inside his coat, Meagan's arm made some motions then came to rest. Bedders knew Meagan had freed his pistol and had it hidden but ready beneath the heavy pelts. They rode up at a trot, stopping ten feet from the visitors, who had abandoned their snooping and lined up. Each had a rifle across his saddle like their boss.

Danelles waited quietly, his squat face reddened by the

cold, scowling deeply with anger. The moon was strong and he squinted against the glare of snow spread in a thin blanket over frozen mud.

'Terrible weather for neighbours to come a-callin', Pistol Nate,' Meagan said, grinning. Already the tenor of this meeting had been set by Meagan's foolish bravado. Several of Danelles' men bristled at the comment.

'We ain'ta here fer neighbouring, Meagan.' Danelles glanced over at Bedders. 'This ain't fer you, young fella. I think I read ya well enough, an' I don'ta believe yer in this with him.'

'If you're here for more than just talk, Mr Danelles I may have to side with Abel.'

'Hell! Ain'ta nothin' gonna happen – if'n he's reasonable, that is.'

Grinning, Meagan said, 'I'm always reasonable.' His gaze shifted over the line of men toward the valley mouth. A rider was coming in hard, scattering cold-lazy cows out of his path. Meagan's grin widened and took on a harder edge.

The others heard the approach of another horse now and tentatively turned in their saddles. It was Jimmy Christopher. He leapt his horse over the creek and came to Meagan's side, the animal steaming all over its body.

'Visitors, Mr Meagan?' He wore the same cruel smile as his boss.

'They came to jaw. Go ahead and speak your piece, Danelles.'

Danelles' men were noticeably agitated now. Two of them had cocked their rifles as Christopher thundered by them. They wore the hard, determined look of men ready to kill.

'Jes' had a couple hundred head stolen from my winter

range,' Danelles told Meagan. 'I think ya had somethin' to do with it.'

Meagan was about to speak but Bedders cut him off. 'No, sir. Not today. Meagan has been with me all after-noon.'

'He's got men, don't he?' one of Danelles' crew said. It was the blond from town who had set up the dry gulch attempt. He cast a glance at Bedders. 'Maybe you really are one of 'em.'

'Heard tell of a fellow in town today,' Christopher said, casually, 'who called another fella out and then ran away when shots were fired. He was pale as a girl, so they say.'

The blond man started to bring his rifle up. 'Don't, Cavell. I'm handlin' this,' Danelles ordered.

'They say the wind was howling as he ran,' Christopher continued, egging the blond, Cavell, on. 'Or maybe it was just that fella crying.'

'Enough! He's right, Meagan, you've got men. Where's that dumb lug you used to have around?'

'Baxter? He lit out months ago. And unless I miss my guess that's Lefferts in my cabin, probably drinking my whiskey.'

There was a warm, red glow leaking out from Meagan's cabin across the creek.

'And Christopher?'

'I was around,' Christopher answered.

'Fact is, I just hired the poor fella. Couldn't bear to see a man stuck out in this cold without a job or a place to sleep or warm grub. He's been riding herd on my other range.'

Danelles boiled. 'Ya mean my range, ya thief! Ye've been a-crowdin' me for like unto a year now. And I've had enough of it.'

'They shot Dan this afternoon, too,' Cavell said, biting his lip, his fingers squeezing the rifle stock.

'You know what happened there, Cavell,' Bedders said. 'You set it up to backshoot Meagan.'

'Better'n he deserves!'

'Cavell, shut up. Dan got what he deserved fer that fool stunt. I'm talkin' about cows.'

'Well, I didn't take them.' Meagan was the picture of innocence.

'Maybe this time, and I don't own to that. But there's been other times. I figure I've lost five hundred head or more. And I've come for satisfaction.'

'Mr Danelles,' said Bedders, 'you've got a grievance. This isn't the way to resolve it. Get a marshal, or ask the Fremont County sheriff to come in.'

'Don't need no sheriff. Now I come for my cattle. I can figure which are mine from that bollixed job of brandin' ye've done.'

'Ain't nothing to figure, old man,' Meagan said. There was a dangerous edge in his voice now. Beside him Christopher had brought a pistol up over his saddle horn. 'None of these cows is yours. You best be moving on.'

'Yer the one who'll be a-travelin' when we're done with ya.'

In a flash of movement, Bedders reined his horse over and into Meagan's. Leaning out of the saddle he swung his right arm over, a coil of rope suddenly in his hand, and slapped the flank of Christopher's mount. The horse reared up kicking in reckless fright and spun on its hind legs. Christopher fired a shot that went wide, plucking at the edge of Danelles' coat.

Frightened, Meagan's horse tried to turn away but found it was boxed in by Christopher's crazed animal and

Bedders' piebald. It reared up, tossing Meagan to the hard ground.

Another shot rang out. Bedders heard an insect-like buzz pass by his ear. He threw himself to the hard ground, rolled to his feet, and slapped again at Christopher's horse. The animal bolted and ran.

'Hold yer fire!' Danelles cried.

Bedders turned and saw a frozen tableau. To his mind, it still looked like a lit fuse on a keg of dynamite. A chill passed through him as he realized Danelles' men wanted blood now.

Meagan was on the ground, cursing and sweeping his hand about trying to reach his gun or the Winchester that had fallen from his saddle scabbard.

'Put up yer guns, fools!'

The men hesitated, all except Cavell. He saw Meagan helpless on the ground and levelled his rifle. Leaning up in the saddle he cocked the weapon, then died with an evil grin plastered on his face.

Bedders stood over Meagan, smoking pistol in his hand, unaware of how it had gotten there or even that it had fired the bullet that killed Cavell.

Cavell tumbled from the saddle in absolute silence, thudding heavily to the hard ground. Danelles got down and looked at the dead man. Bedders had put a bullet into the bridge of Cavell's nose.

'Pick him up,' Danelles ordered through clenched teeth. 'Put him across his saddle.'

Several of the men climbed down to do the job.

His horse under control again, Christopher galloped back to the line, grinning, gun at the ready. Bedders reached down and swept up the fallen rifle from the ground then, in the same motion, swung it back to catch

115

Christopher in the gut. The man grunted with pain and shock and tumbled to the frozen earth, cursing.

'Enough!' Bedders screamed. 'Mr Danelles, call the law. But don't come here again looking for this kind of trouble.'

Danelles climbed back into his saddle slowly. 'I guess ye've chosen sides, son.'

When they were gone Meagan got to his feet, laughing and slapping snow from his coat.

'Well, pard, I guess you're in it now.'

'Is that all you've got to say!'

Meagan thought for a moment then shrugged. 'I suppose I should thank you for saving me the trouble of shooting that fella.'

Bedders spun and slammed a fist into Meagan's face, knocking the man down again.

'I just shot a man, Abel. Killed him. For you. Because of you.'

Rubbing his jaw, Meagan said, 'Well, we're pards, ain't we?'

'No. We're not. You damned fool. You killed that the first day we got to this valley. You didn't want a partner. So now you don't have one. And you don't have a friend.'

'Then why'd you kill him, Nix? Whyn't ya just let the blond bag of wind plug me and be rid of me.'

Bedders climbed on to the piebald, his head hung low. 'I – I don't know,' he said, then kicked the animal into a gallop.

'You want me to go after him?' Christopher asked.

Meagan shook his head slowly. 'No. There's time enough later.'

Bedders had little sleep that night. He faced no nightmares, no ghosts in the dark. But his thoughts were so

116

jumbled, his emotions so agitated, that his mind would not let him rest. He had spent his life bouncing from place to place, never settling, interested in nothing but the freedom of the wandering trail he travelled. Meagan had been right that day, he was a stone rolling down hill. Twice in his past he had stumbled into other men's fights. He had been young and foolish, not recognizing the telltale signs of scowling faces and quick guns. When he had awakened to the trouble surrounding him, he had left. Not out of cowardice but simply because it hadn't been his fight. To fight meant that you had to care for something, and that you would stay around after the fighting was done. He hadn't wanted to stay in one place. The trail called to him like a siren and he had been powerless to resist.

Things were different now. He did care. About this valley, his neighbours, the folks in Lander. What they thought of him mattered a lot. And then there was Emily. God, what would she think of him now?

Closing his eyes he imagined a giant black maw closing in on him, devouring him. He had defended his friend, but it felt like murder.

The country would band against Meagan, now, and they would probably be careless in their zeal to rid the area of him. Cavanaugh would be enlisted, some of the other, smaller ranchers, too. That last fleeting look Danelles had tossed at them, so hateful and full of the promise of revenge.

If Meagan was a rustler, he should be punished, Bedders thought. But by the law, not by the gun or rope. He owed his friend nothing, really. Nothing but fairness.

At dawn, his eyes blurry and red, Bedders decided to go to Cavanaugh and plead his case. The rancher carried a lot of weight in the area. He would get the law, he would see that honest justice was done. Trembling, Bedders realized he needed Cavanaugh to do it because he couldn't. In his mind such would be a betrayal to his childhood friend.

Bedders had just saddled the piebald when Meagan rode up.

'Nix, I need to talk with you.'

'I gotta go,' Bedders said, not looking at the man.

'I know I did wrong, Nix. But I need you now. I need my friend.' Bedders could hear honest desperation in Meagan's voice. He looked up and saw Meagan sported bleary eyes, as well.

'They're pushin' us back, Nix. What critters they haven't run off, they're pushin' back into the valley.'

'That's where your stock should be.'

'I ain't got enough grass for 'em all, Nix. I need more grass.'

Bedders hung his head and found the strength to squeeze out the word. 'No.'

'I gotta have it, or they'll all of 'em die.'

'Cross that creek with your stock, Meagan, and I'll kill you.'

Waiting for no reply, Bedders hopped aboard the piebald and galloped toward the valley mouth.

Bedders had been to the Cavanaugh spread only once before, what seemed like ages ago when he helped the rancher to drive in his new herd of long horns. The house was actually modest in size, low to the ground and solidly built of stone and logs. Around it was built a wide porch and several stone chimneys that belched white smoke. There was a warm glow about the place as Bedders approached.

Passing through an open, arched gate, Bedders saw two

barns, several corrals, a long bunkhouse for the ranch hands, and a cookshack. To left of the main house was a fenced-in area that had the remnants of a truck garden, now covered in snow. Dogs barked as he approached, snapping at the piebald's heels.

A few of the ranch hands ventured out into the cold, curious. Cavanaugh himself came to the door, framed in a yellow-orange glow. He stood for a long time with his arms folded, the lines on his face creased deeply about his eyes and mouth.

'Step down and come inside,' he said eventually.

Bedders tied the piebald to a post, climbed the few steps to the porch, and shuffled into the house. In a glance he noticed the heavy furniture upholstered in horsehair and the stone fireplace blazing at the back of the low-ceilinged room. A man sitting in a chair now stood and left the room.

'You must have gotten an early start – have you eaten?'

Bedders shook his head. 'I don't want to impose, Mr Cavanaugh. I just want to talk.'

'A man's gotta eat. Come on.'

Cavanaugh turned and walked down a short hallway to a large dining room, at the centre of which was a massive mahogany table polished to a brilliant sheen. He pushed open a door and leaned in, thick cooking aromas escaping into the room. There was a girl at the stove, Cavanaugh's daughter, Sarah. She was a pretty girl of sixteen with dark hazel eyes and a thick mane of black hair. Beside her in an apron was an old Mexican woman.

'Sarah, got a man here needs breakfast.'

'Breakfast is at six, father, you know that,' she said teasingly as she turned. When she saw her father's stern face and glimpsed Bedders through the doorway her smile vanished to be replaced by childlike curiosity.

'Just bring us something, please.'

Cavanaugh let the door swing closed then motioned for Bedders to take a seat. The chair was large and cushioned but the young man couldn't seem to get comfortable.

'I suppose you know what happened yesterday with one of Danelles' men,' Bedders said.

'I heard what happened to two of his men,' Cavanaugh corrected. 'Both of them shot by you. Tell me about it.'

Bedders nodded. He told the story unvarnished, exactly as it had occurred. Cavanaugh said nothing, but twice he nodded with silent understanding. Sarah came into the room and put a plate of eggs and a steak in front of him, along with a bowl of bread and a jar of jam. She poured coffee into two mugs and gave one to her father. All the while she looked on Bedders with a girlish appreciation and wonder. Oblivious, Bedders ate and talked until he was done.

Cavanaugh was silent for a minute then said, 'Told 'em we needed a marshal in town. You wouldn't want the job, would you, son?'

He had asked in jest and grunted a laugh at how quickly Bedders declined.

'Do you know why I came to you that day and asked you drive a herd with me?'

'No, sir.'

'I did it because your friend is trouble. I saw that right off. But I didn't think you were. I thought you were here to build a good life, to start a ranch not trouble. I knew that I'd rather have you for a neighbour than Meagan.'

'Haven't been much of a neighbour, I expect.'

'No, son. You've kept your head in the sand. Well, we all have, I guess. Meagan was smart. He took only a few head at a time so we'd hardly notice. And if we did see it, we didn't want to care.' Cavanaugh paused to look into the kitchen. Sarah had slyly left the door open. For a moment he watched his young daughter, busy at a table cutting vegetables, happy and healthy and unafraid. 'Certainly not enough to send us down a killing path again. This country's been through that years ago, and there's no one wants to live it all again.'

'I think Danelles is ready.'

Cavanaugh agreed. He took a sip of his coffee, reluctant to say what else was on his mind.

'I saw something that first day, Bedders. Something bad that would happen. It would take time for it to develop, but I saw then it was inevitable.'

Already knowing the answer, the young man asked, 'What was it?'

'I saw that you and Meagan were going to have to square off against each other. I knew then that your small valley would be a tomb for one of you. He's hungry. Well, you both are, only I don't suppose you really know it. But it was his hunger I was afraid of. He wanted it all, and more. You're going to have to stop him, Bedders, because if you don't he's going to come after me next and I'll kill him before he can make that move.'

Cavanaugh glanced again at his daughter in the kitchen then got up and left the room.

Sleep came to Bedders that night not from relief but from exhaustion. Arriving home in the evening he saw to the piebald's needs and its warmth then went inside and stoked the fire beneath the pot of beans on the stove. As he ate, with his eyes drooping, he thought longingly of Emily's cooking. He fell asleep by the fire with his hat for a pillow and a horse blanket to cover him.

He awoke with a start in utter darkness and cold. The fire had died. For a moment only the whistling wind could be heard in the still night. Something had jarred him from sleep, something other than cold. Cautiously he stood and felt his way to the shuttered window.

Now he heard the piebald stamping and snorting nervously. Agitated cows were mewling in the distance. Bedders thought for a moment, still groggy, trying to remember where he had placed his Remington when he came in. Feeling around for it he found his saddle and then the rifle. Back at the window he unloosed the latch and swung the shutters open slowly.

A bright moon obscured by clouds hung over the south ridge and cast its ghostly glow down into the valley. It was a pale light, illuminating little, but out of the corner of his eye Bedders sensed that the cattle were on the move.

He went outside, his nerve endings jangling, waiting for the crack of a rifle. He found the piebald stamping inside the lean-to he had built for it, nervously tossing its head. Bedders spoke to it quietly as he threw the saddle on to its back. A few cows passed close by just as Bedders was about to turn the piebald. He froze seeing a horse and rider, merely a shadow in the black night, following behind the stock, pushing them along.

After they passed, Bedders mounted and rode away from his house, deeper into the valley. He found a couple of cows and, rounding them up, pushed them in the direction of the other rider. He pulled his hat low on his face and held the Remington, loaded and cocked, across his saddle horn.

He rode toward the creek and as he rounded Apple Rock he could make out a sea of cows before him, an undulating shadow under pale, filtered moonlight. Anger grew in him. Meagan was rustling from him, now, a last desperate act as he prepared to escape with his stolen herd.

'Didn't have many on that side of the range,' someone said, the wind carrying the sound to Bedders. He glanced to his right and saw two men on horseback pressed close to one another.

'Don't matter.' Neither of the voices belonged to Meagan.

There were three other riders that he could see, their dark shadows rising above the black sea of cows. Meagan only had two men. Well, Bedders thought, it was easy enough to buy cheap men. Then he saw two more riders and realized Meagan was not the one orchestrating this night roundup. This was Danelles' doing.

'Bring 'em over here,' a voice whispered. Bedders had started to ride away when the voice called out to him. He was trapped. If he turned now they would know he wasn't one of them.

Bedders pushed the cows ahead of him, keeping his head low. He mingled in with the herd and allowed them to edge him away from the other riders.

'Out to the valley mouth,' the voice said.

The words had just floated up to Bedders when the night erupted in sudden gunfire. The animals cried out in terror and began to stampede. But they were facing in all directions and ran into each other. Their panic grew. A horse collapsed in the crush of bodies and the rider fell, screaming.

A constant stream of gunfire echoed off the limestone face of the valley.

Bedders edged the piebald toward the small protection of a rock that jutted out from the sheer valley wall. From his vantage he could just make out two other riders racing across the valley, firing rifles and screaming wildly. Bedders recognized Meagan's voice.

Two of the riders broke away from the herd and charged Meagan. They fired and Meagan literally flew from the saddle.

Instantly, Bedders spurred the piebald forward into a gallop, sliding his rifle into its scabbard. He charged across the range using his pistol to send warning shots at the two riders. Confused, they turned away.

Bedders forced his way through the panicking herd and found Meagan on the ground, groaning.

'Come on!'

Moaning painfully, Meagan stood, took hold of Bedders' arm, and pulled himself up on to the piebald. The horse grunted at the double load, snorting as its own panic began to rise in the crush of animals. Bedders reined over and sent the horse out of the milling bunch.

More shots were fired. Like a switch, something clicked with the herd and they all turned and began racing off deep into the valley, a deadly, pounding swarm. Several of the riders turned and raced for the safety of the pass to Lander.

The piebald gained the rock, slipping in behind it. After the herd thundered past, Bedders kicked his horse into a gallop and raced for his cabin. He dragged Meagan inside and lit a lantern.

'Who are they?' Meagan asked, breathless. He was holding his shoulder where blood seeped out through his fingers.

Several more shots rang out.

'Danelles' men, I think,' Bedders told him. 'Who was that with you?'

'Christopher. He'll kill 'em.'

Leaving Meagan behind, Bedders ran for the piebald and chased after the escaping men. He was close enough to see several men disappear down the pass, followed quickly by another.

The moon's pale light barely touched the narrow pass. Blind, Bedders let the horse find its way by instinct. He could hear the pounding of hoofs ahead of him. A few shots cracked and echoed in the narrow confines of the pass, then pinged off the sheer rock face. Bedders heard a man cry out and thud to the ground. Moments later the piebald screamed as it lost its footing and tumbled. Bedders threw himself from the saddle blindly and smacked against a rock. He hit his head and his left shoulder crunched against something unmoving. He lay still for a moment listening to the dull sound of horses' hoofs galloping away.

Then he heard the piebald whimper in pain. He felt his way over to the animal. It was lying on its side and jumped at his touch. It was in a great deal of pain.

'Sorry, boy,' he said as he fired two shots into the horse's head.

He was close to town and despite the pain in his head and shoulder he ran. What Danelles and his men had done this night had been wrong. But Christopher killing those men would escalate things beyond redemption. He had to be stopped.

'Help me!' a voice called out.

'Who's there?'

'Ebberly from Danelles' outfit.'

There was a thin shadow in the rocks. 'Toss out your guns,' Bedders said.

'I lost 'em.'

'So help me, you. . . .'

'I ain't got 'em, I tell you.'

Bedders found the man propped up against a rock, grunting as he tried to shift his body. 'Think I broke my leg.'

'Damn lucky that's all you got.'

'Yeah. My horse is up ahead. Bring it around so I can get aboard.'

Bedders heard the animal stamping lightly on the frozen earth. 'I'll be back for you.'

'You can't leave me!'

'I won't. I'll be back for you!'

The horse hadn't fallen and nervous as it was it leapt into a gallop as Bedders climbed aboard and carried him to town quickly. Lights were still lit in many of the houses and the several saloons along the main street. He slowed the horse to a walk, scanning both sides of the street for lathered horses. He found two of them in an alley next to the Owl Creek saloon. He saw a shadow move across the saloon's lone lighted window then push on through the low front door. Bedders jumped off the horse and charged inside.

Christopher was there with two guns drawn. He fired wildly into the dark back corner of the saloon where several men sat playing cards. The men scattered, diving for the floor. Christopher screamed maniacally and fired again.

Bedders leapt forward and grabbed Christopher around the arms, forcing the guns down. The weapons fired unintentionally, blasting holes beside the man's boots. Squeezing, Bedders lifted the man then slammed him forward into the edge of the bar. With a great sigh, Christopher doubled over.

Bedders slapped the guns from the man's hands then punched him hard in the face. Christopher dropped to one knee, his head bobbing slightly. Breathing heavily Bedders took a half step back, fist balled, barely in control of his anger. Suddenly, Christopher was on his feet. He rammed a fist into Bedders' gut even as Bedders swung a leaden hand against the side of his head. There was a crazed look in Christopher's eyes, an insane joy for killing.

Bedders fell to the dusty floor. As he fell he kicked out with his boots, scissoring Christopher's legs. The man jerked and tumbled, catching a hand on the edge of the bar. Bedders rolled and instinctively reached for his gun. But Christopher had no weapon and he hesitated.

Christopher sensed the doubt and leapt at Bedders. The two men tumbled, a sharp splinter from the floor gouging Bedders' cheek. They rolled and the gunman came up on top, but only for a second. Before Christopher could slam a quick fist home, Bedders' hand found a beer mug that had fallen to the floor and swept it against Christopher's head. The gunman screamed as blood spurted from a gash near his eye. He threw himself to the floor, screaming in pain. But it was a ruse. He lunged toward his fallen guns, grabbed one, and had just started to spin back toward Bedders when a boot caught him in the head and sent him in a heap to the floor. Bedders stepped on Christopher's gun hand, grinding his heel until the man screamed.

Something snapped in Bedders then, a horrible rage took control of him. He lifted Christopher to his feet and hit him again, and he kept hitting the man until the vicious ranch hand collapsed into a bloody, pulpy pile on the dirty floor.

Knuckles red and painfully swelling, Bedders stepped

back. His Colt was in his hand now, summoned unconsciously there. The barrel wavered slightly between Christopher's head and his heart. Breathing great gulps of air it took a minute before Bedders could speak.

'No more killing,' he said.

Christopher tried to rise up on an elbow but couldn't. He collapsed like a limp rag and rolled on to his back. 'You've made an enemy today,' he said, his ragged speech slurring. His lips were cracked and bloody. A tooth had been knocked loose and it looked as if his entire mouth had been permanently twisted from the beating.

'No, Christopher, it's you who's made an enemy. Get out of this country. Right now. Because the next time I see you, you're a dead man.'

CHAPTER NINE

Snowmelt and spring rains had swollen the creek and the small pond at the centre of the valley into a rushing gout of icy water overflowing its shallow banks. Meagan's side of the valley was a quagmire of mud and brown grass and dead cattle. Dozens of cows lay where they had fallen last winter in the aborted stampede, frozen at first and now rotting, their rancid smell hung like a pall over that end of the valley. Meagan had not tried to move the animals. He had retreated to his meagre home, wounded and surly, spending his time recuperating and nursing bitterness.

The weather was warming now and tufts of green grass were beginning to grow, but no sooner did a few shoots sprout than the ravenous cows ate them. Danelles and his men had made certain that Meagan's cattle stayed within the valley, and now the land was nearly played out. They had taken some of the herd, those that had wandered outside the valley. But Danelles was not willing to risk any more of his men in another attempted raid. Meagan would be gone soon enough, he believed, and what belonged to Danelles would be returned to him.

Still, several of Danelles' men came to the mouth of the valley, venturing in only a little, and taunting Meagan with gunshots. That had gone on all winter, and Bedders had let it. It was childish, he knew, but he believed that Meagan was finished and the taunting would not bait a foolish, deadly reaction by the man who had once been his friend.

He had seen Meagan taunted many times. He never retaliated, never lashed out, never did anything foolish. Funny, Bedders thought, to remember something like that now. Meagan had taken a lot of abuse back in Spearman as a youth. A scrawny kid, orphaned and seemingly timid, many of the boys in town had taken turns baiting and beating Meagan. Had he, Bedders, ever done anything to stop it? Thinking back, he did remember stepping in front of a few fists. He had put an arm around Meagan, too, declaring their friendship. Young as he was, he thought that would settle things. He realized now that it hadn't. Bedders' friendship hadn't been enough to protect Meagan back then, and it wasn't enough now. This trouble was something Meagan had to deal with alone.

How easily the past and the present melded together, Bedders thought, pausing above the chopping block, axe in hand, back dripping with sweat and enjoying the first hint of spring weather. The distant, lonely crack of a rifle lifted to him on a soft breeze. More taunting. Meagan had made this bed; he'd have to sleep in it.

Still, this part of the country had been badly damaged by their arrival. Not for the first time during the long winter months a wave of depression washed over Bedders. For much of the day he had set about chopping wood, trying in vain not to think about what he had done by bringing Meagan here. Somehow he had to square things with the ranchers and the people of Lander. Cavanaugh had said it was up to Bedders to rid the country of Meagan. Sweat trickling down his neck, again swinging the axe with grim determination, Bedders knew Cavanaugh had been right. But to confront Meagan would mean he'd have to shoot him, and he couldn't do that. He could not kill his friend, no matter what the man had done.

There had to be another way.

That night it came to him. Most of the ranchers believed Meagan had cattle, stolen from them, hidden in the hills surrounding the valley. Men like Lincoln had spent a great deal of time searching for hidden canyons large enough to temporarily hold a few hundred head. If Bedders could find those cattle and return them to their owners Meagan would lose a source of income. His herd wouldn't survive the summer on his range and it would force Meagan to make a drive. Once out of the valley, he'd never be let back in.

But would the ranchers let it go at that. With a sinking feeling, Bedders knew they wouldn't. They would track Meagan and steal back their stock. Meagan would be forced to fight and he would die. A quiet voice reminded that Meagan had made this bed. Bedders cursed the voice and went to sleep.

The following morning he rounded up a white mare to ride and a mouse-brown packhorse and filled leather pouches with supplies. He would find Meagan's ill-gotten herd and return it to the rightful owners. Maybe that would give him leverage enough with the angry ranchers to see Meagan's life spared.

There were several dozen passages that branched off of the main route from the valley to the town of Lander. All of these had been searched, Bedders knew, for he had seen men roaming through them, most notably Lincoln. The big, craggy-faced man had spent days wandering the limestone hills, scratching his way through narrow passes

and into tight box canyons. Bedders had seen him several
times as he rode to town and each time Lincoln had
grinned deathlike at him. He meant to kill Meagan and
hadn't only because Cavanaugh held his leash.

In the opposite direction there was a short range of low,
rolling hills at the foot of the Granite Ridges, a series of
rough-carved bluffs that separated Cavanaugh's land from
Danelles'. Beyond that, outside Fremont County, were the
Rattlesnake Hills that rose up on scraggly, crooked backs,
twisting around small streams and shadowing for a long
stretch the Sweetwater River. It would be a gutsy move to
run stolen cattle into that range, cutting between the two
largest ranchers in the territory. From there, though, if he
had found passage through the range, he could have
gotten his stolen cattle to market easily. Meagan was clever,
Bedders knew, but he wondered if the man was daring
enough to act on such a scheme.

Nudging his horse forward, he led the pack animal out
of the valley. As he neared the valley mouth he felt eyes on
him, watching his movements. He resisted the urge to turn
around and glance back at Meagan's cabin, at the window
from which curious eyes watched. Other eyes were on
Bedders, too, as he crossed open range and climbed the
low hills. The centre of his back itched with anticipation of
a bullet that never came.

Out of the hills, Bedders crossed more open land. He
made camp that night by a small creek, only a few miles from
the low mountain range. The next morning he rode along
the base of the Rattlesnake Hills searching for canyon passes
at the scabrous base of the range. In the first few hours he
found nearly a dozen passes that lead nowhere. That afternoon he circled the range south, the Sweetwater River rushing below him at the bottom of gently sloping hills.

For four days he searched and found nothing. There were hundreds, perhaps thousands of breaks in the mountain range, most of them no deeper than a few dozen feet, or wider than the width of a man on horseback. The amount of area to cover was huge. Without knowing more, Bedders realized he wouldn't be able to find what he was looking for.

He rode back, dejected, the overwhelming feeling of impotence weighing him down. It had been a foolish plan, he decided, cursing himself. He would have to confront Meagan directly. It was something he should have done a long time ago, he told himself, feeling imbued with new wisdom. No, not wisdom. Just the lifting, finally, of a dark veil from before his eyes.

Yet as he neared his valley he could not bring himself to enter it. Instead, he rode on to Lander, cutting uneventfully through Cavanaugh's land. He didn't know it until he got to her door as dusk was settling over the town, but he needed to see Emily.

The office was closed. He went around back, hoping to find her working late, but saw the lights were off. Leading his horse, he walked to the Pattersons' modest home in the next street, set behind a wrought iron fence on a small plot of land. The house was built of weathered red brick and blackened window frames. There was a small porch at the right and a large bay window covered with soft drapes.

Emily opened the door for him in a rush and fell into his arms. He kissed her without thinking, then pushed her away. She refused to be moved and stepped back into his arms and kissed him again.

'It ain't healthy to be my friend, I think,' he told her, profound sadness in his face.

'Being young doesn't give you a licence to be foolish,

boy,' John Patterson called. 'Come in, if my daughter will let go of you long enough to set your boots inside.'

Emily blushed prettily and stepped aside for Bedders to enter. Sweeping his hat off he stammered, 'I'm sorry to barge in, sir.'

'Nonsense. You haven't been to town in months,' Patterson said. 'Things have been down right quiet.'

'Oh, Dad.'

Emily showed him into the living room and sat him in a large chair, settling herself on its upholstered arm. Patterson was in his wheelchair next to a side table with a large oil lamp at his elbow.

'We've had our supper, but I'm sure Emily can rustle up something for you.'

Bedders said he couldn't eat, but he accepted an offer of coffee. Emily rushed off to the kitchen to get some.

'I've been looking for where Meagan has stashed those stolen cattle.' Patterson paused in lighting his pipe to look at the young man over the flaming match. Then he began to puff rhythmically, drawing the heat on to the tobacco.

'A lot of men have been doing that,' he said.

'I guess that's right. I've seen Lincoln more than a few times scouring the hills.'

Emily brought the coffee and they all sat in silence drinking it for a time.

'You know now that Meagan is stealing cattle?'

'I guess I knew that all along.' Bedders reddened more out of anger than embarrassment. 'He was my friend. I didn't want to believe ill of him.'

'We understand, Morton.' Emily came to him, again sitting on the arm of the chair. The heat of her nearness quickened his pulse, clouded his mind.

'If I can find those cattle and return them Meagan will

have to leave and maybe folks won't want to kill him.'

'Maybe. Some of the boys will want to kill him anyway. Him and that Christopher fella. But they're going about it right. They're getting the sheriff involved or, if that don't work, they'll hire a town marshal. Either way, Meagan is finished. The only question is does he leave a-horseback or in a pine box.'

Despite having had the same thoughts, Patterson's words hit Bedders like a blow to the stomach. There was something so brutal in the man's simple statement. So final.

'They've sent for the sheriff, then?'

'Not yet. They're deciding that now down at the Owl Creek.'

Bedders' eyes narrowed. 'You're not down there with them?'

'No, son. Been waiting for you to come around and take care of things. Cavanaugh was waiting, too. But not any more. He's with that crowd now.'

Rising to his feet he found Emily by his side.

'Don't go, Morton. Please.'

'I have to face this. Try to make things right.'

'It's not your fault. Not really.'

'No, I don't think it is. Not any more. This is Meagan's doing. But I brought him here. I can't disown that.'

He took her in his arms and kissed her again, mindless of her father's presence. When he had gone, Patterson said, 'Well, it's about time he did that proper.'

Her face crimsoning, she ran to the window to watch Bedders march down the street.

Rounding the corner, Bedders saw several men entering the Owl Creek. More than two dozen horses were tied at the rails outside the saloon. He mounted the steps to the walk then pushed his way through the tall front doors. Smoke hung in a brownish haze over a crush of men all facing the back of the room where a man was standing on a chair. He had his hands raised and was trying to be heard over the angry babble of the mob.

A man entered the saloon after Bedders, his heavy foot-steps thudding on the wood, and brushed by him roughly.

'Mr Danelles!' Bedders called, recognizing the man.

Agitated, Danelles had seen nothing in front of him and looked now as if he was waking from a dream as he saw Bedders.

'Go home, young fella. This ain't no place fer you.'

Bedders took gentle hold of Danelles' arm. 'Please, Mr Danelles let me say something.'

Danelles' entrance had disrupted the confusion at the front of the room, attracting the attention of some of the men.

'Hey, there's the other one!' someone called out.

A man grabbed Bedders from behind, pinning his arms. Another stepped forward and, grinning like a rabid ferret, slammed a fist into Bedders' gut. A third man joined in sending a punch across Bedders' face. Danelles threw himself into the mêlée, pushing the men away.

'Stop it, you men! Leave him be!'

Cavanaugh came forward and began peeling the riotous men away.

'That's enough from all of you!' he declared in a room that had finally gone silent. 'You shouldn't be here, Bedders.'

'I have to be. You're all getting set to kill a man. Oh, you'll couch it in the law because you're all fine, upstand-ing citizens. But it's little more than a public hanging is what you're after.'

'You forgettin' he killed one 'a my men?' Danelles reminded.

'He didn't do that. I did. I killed him because he was looking for blood and was ready to gun down an unarmed man. And don't you think you didn't have anything to do with that, either.' Bedders pointed a stern finger at Danelles. 'That hot-headed ranny of yours would still be alive if you hadn't come into the valley looking to shoot it out.'

Danelles' lips compressed into a tight white line. He stared hard at Bedders for a moment then his eyes dropped. 'Cavell was an idiot. But he was killed because my cattle's been stolen.'

'And so you're going to the law,' Bedders scoffed.

'You told us that's what we should do,' one of Danelles' men said.

'Sure. But you don't want justice. You want blood. You're sending for the law so they can do your killing for you. All you want is Meagan dead.'

'Rustling can get you dead, son,' Cavanaugh said, quietly.

'I don't want him dead. He was a friend of mine.'

'Was?'

'Meagan's been wrong. I know that now. But killing him only gets your stock back. And none of you have been hit so hard as to be missing what was stolen. It's a matter of pride. I understand that. A man shouldn't steal. But this killing is wrong.'

'It doesn't have to be like that,' Cavanaugh told him. 'It doesn't have to end in death.'

'It will. You know it will, because he'll fight you.' Bedders turned to face the gathering. 'Let me handle Meagan.'

'Like ya did afore?' someone cried out.

'No! I didn't see what was going on before because I didn't want to. He was my friend. But I see it now. Let me handle him. I'll get him out of this territory, but you've got to leave it to me.'

Danelles came forward, scowling, shaking his head. 'That's jest it, son. We don't trust ya. Some of us ain't so sure where ya stand, and we ain't goin' to wait no more.'

Looking from man to man, Bedders saw the distrust. Some of the men looked away, embarrassed. Maybe they still believed in him. He had made some friends here, yet none of them would speak for him now. Patterson had been right. Things had gone too far for that.

He started to leave but stopped and looked with pleading eyes to Cavanaugh.

'Let me get him out,' Bedders said.

The big rancher shrugged. 'It's too late for that.'

'It doesn't have to be.'

'Go on, son. It's either the law or a lynching. Things have gone too far. There's no other choice now.'

Outside night had fallen and with the darkness came a cold bite to the air. The smell of hay and warm cookstoves scented the evening, clearing Bedders' lungs of the raw saloon smoke. He could hear the laughter of a few of them still inside, the grumbling of others, then it all melded into angry nonsense. Irritated with them, and with himself, Bedders stepped into the street rounding the horses at the rail, his hands stuffed deep into the pockets of his heavy coat.

A shot rang out, the bullet plucking at Bedders' coat sleeve, tugging at his left arm. He dropped to the ground in shock, feeling his arm go numb and a buzzing sound rising in his ears. He fumbled with his gun, dropping it as it cleared the holster. Another shot slapped at the hard ground and sent a gout of dust and pebbles up into the air.

The horses tied to the rail pulled at their reins and whinnied with fear. They began to move nervously, several of them almost stepping on him.

Another shot rang out and a horse screamed then, sensing Bedders' closeness, bucked and nearly kicked him with a deathblow to the head. Bedders' hand found his gun and he rolled into the confusion of jittery horses, some of which had managed to pull loose from the rails and bolt down the dark street.

Up on the walk now, bending low, Bedders sought the cover of a post. Some of the horses still milled nervously at the rail and that gave him some protection, but it also hindered his view of the shooter. The man was across the street and could have been in any of the stores or houses there. The Popo Agie Hotel was directly across from him as well, and all of its windows were dark.

Taking cautious backward steps, Bedders felt for the saloon doors, found them and pushed. Locked! Someone had closed and barred them. There was some yelling going on inside but the words were indistinguishable.

'Over here,' came a harsh whisper.

Bedders dared a quick glance to the end of the walk, toward the black corner of the saloon. Someone was standing there, a dark gun in his hand.

Another shot slapped against the wood of the saloon door. Not hesitating, Bedders threw himself on to the walk and rolled off into the dirt just as another shot chipped the wood planks. Crawling, he found safety in the narrow black alley between the saloon and another building. A hand grabbed him and hauled him to his feet then pressed him against the wall.

'You're the damned luckiest drover I ever met,' the gravely voice said.

'Who are you?'

Bedders sensed the man was smiling. He was big and strong and hard as granite.

'Move,' he said.

He let go of Bedders and stepped around some boxes then made his way to the back of the building. Pale lantern-light from a window cast an orange square on the ground. The man avoided this, but enough light washed over him for Bedders to identify him.

'Lincoln! What are you doing here?' Bedders whispered.

'You want to catch that shooter or don't you?' The crags in his face seemed deeper, almost bloody in the strange glow of the lamplight.

'He's probably gone.'

'Don't count on it. They want you dead, boy. Not just your partner.'

'He's not my partner.'

Lincoln's eyes narrowed. 'He's got you doing his killing.'

'Would you have stood by as Cavell gunned down an unarmed man? Hell, you're helping me now, and I've got a gun.'

'You want this shooter?' Lincoln asked after a long silence.

'Leave him. Like I said, he's probably—'

The loud blast of a gun startled Bedders. The window crashed and the lantern shattered, plunging the alley into darkness. Lincoln's heavy hand grabbed hold of Bedders and dragged him against the wall.

'We'll go around opposite directions,' he ordered in a

hoarse whisper. 'Work our way back to the centre. Get across the street. He's over there somewhere. And for Heaven's sake, don't shoot me.' Lincoln pushed away from the wall with a grunt and crossed the alley.

'Same goes for you.'

'We'll see,' answered the darkness.

Bedders ran to the far end of the building where there was only a very narrow gap between it and a milliner's shop. He thought to squeeze into the space then decided against it; his arm was still numb and was just now beginning to throb. An empty lot sat next to the milliner's shop. Bedders ran to this and using the cover of a broken down wagon and several cracked barrels made his way to the street.

Light from half a dozen windows filtered out on to the street making weird shadows. The town had gone quiet. Whatever ruckus there had been in the Owl Creek had been put down. Waiting in the darkness Bedders let his mind wander. Someone in the saloon had planned this attack. A man outside to do the killing and a man inside to hold the others at bay. Danelles' name sprang to mind, but others might have done it. In the end, it didn't matter. The country seemed lined up against him and he wondered if getting rid of Meagan would redeem him. He wondered, too, if he even wanted redemption at that price.

A shadow too small to be Lincoln moved along the opposite walk, paused beside a post, then ducked into an alley. Bedders ran across the street, keeping low with his gun before him, ready. At the corner he peered into the darkness, saw a fleeting image at the end of the alley disappearing behind a house, and followed for two more houses.

The orange, spurting flame of a pistol shot flashed

suddenly, the crack of the gun and the pinging ricochet sounding at the same instant. Bedders ducked without returning fire. When he peeked out from behind a fence, the shadow was gone. Bedders ran forward ready to dive to safety, his body awkwardly angled as he nursed his wound. The numbness in his arm had all but gone, replaced by a painful pounding at his shoulder. He flexed the muscles tenderly, then pressed on.

Down the back alley, the door to the livery barn was open an inviting crack. Bedders watched it for a few minutes, deciding. Finally, he came out from behind cover and crossed to it, keeping an eye on the two windows facing him as well as the door. At the door he paused again, listening, then thrust it open. When no shot came, he stepped inside.

Blackness instantly enveloped him, and he was grateful for it. Waiting, back pressed against the rough wooden plank wall, Bedders listened for breathing other than his own. He heard nothing.

He had been in this stable several times but couldn't remember where the stalls were. Only a sliver of light cut into the barn from a small window up in the loft. It fell across the wooden half-wall of a stall and on to a rack of harnesses and saddles. A little bit of light bled off and Bedders could just make out the vertical lines of a fixed ladder to the loft.

He was about to take a step toward the ladder when a hand fell lightly on his gun arm and a voice whispered a barely audible 'Wait.'

Bedders tensed instinctively, then fought back the pounding fear and desire to strike out. He crouched low with a sudden movement and felt rather than saw Lincoln beside him.

'Back in the stalls,' Lincoln said in his ear. Now Bedders could see a shadowy arm pointing. 'Go left. Keep under the light. I'll go right.'

Lincoln did not wait for a reply but simply disappeared. Bedders kept low and took slow steps to the left as he ducked under the pale beam of light that fell to the straw-covered floor. Hearing a gentle crunch, Bedders stopped with a jolt, holding his breath. He could hear soft footfalls to his right where he believed that Lincoln had gone.

Somewhere above them came the sound of a sudden scrape and a rush of wind. Lincoln fired a shot then grunted and moaned in pain. Heavy boots thudded above in the loft. Bedders fired three quick shots. Outside several horses screamed in fear. Bedders ran to the back of the barn, feeling around the walls, desperately looking for an exit. He found a small door and threw it open in time to see a horse and rider galloping out of the corral and back among the low hills that swelled behind the town.

'Lincoln!' Bedders called.

'Get a light,' the ranch foreman moaned.

Bedders went to the front door and pushed it open, then found the large double barn doors and shoved these wide, too. Enough light filtered through the dusty barn for Bedders to find a lantern. Once lit he saw a large bale of hay, trussed up in chicken wire, sitting awkwardly in the middle of the barn floor. Pinned beneath it was Lincoln. With his good shoulder Bedders shoved at the bale until it fell away.

'I'll get a doctor,' Bedders told him.

'No, it's all right. Knocked the wind from me, that's all.'

Lincoln got to his feet, wobbling a little. Bedders held his good arm out to steady the man. Lincoln laughed.

'Maybe you ought to get a doc for yourself,' he said.

'It'll be fine.'

Lincoln peeled Bedders' coat off of him then twisted the arm around into the light. Bedders yelped.

'Hey!'

'Bullet just grazed you,' Lincoln announced. 'Keep it clean and covered with a dry cloth. You'll be fine.' He helped Bedders back into his coat, then said, 'Maybe you'd better find a place to stay in town tonight. That gunman might be waiting for you on the trail back.'

'He went the other way.'

His voice laced with suspicion, Lincoln asked, 'Which way?'

'South. Toward Cavanaugh land.'

After parting with Lincoln, Bedders found his horse at Emily's house, still tied to the hitch rail. Wearily, he climbed aboard. With a longing look, he gazed at Emily's front door. How easy it would be to knock on that door, ask for shelter. But he didn't want to bring any more trouble down on the Pattersons. A lot of folks were lined up against him. He didn't want Emily hurt because of him.

Several times during the ride back to his cabin he nodded off in the saddle, yet the horse managed to find its way and got him home safely. Removing the saddle, he let it lay where it had fallen, having no strength to attend to it. He slapped at the horse to get it into the lean-to and shoved a few handfuls of hay on to the ground. That was all he could do this night. Tomorrow he would face Meagan. They would fight, he knew, and the shame of that weighed heavy on him as he slept fitfully. He should have been able to stop the trouble before it started, he told himself, but now the only way for this to end would be in violence.

CHAPTER TEN

Bedders struggled to rise against a deep sleep that had dulled him. His head felt foggy, as if it were enshrouded in a thick, gritty mist. He coughed a few times, pushing himself on to one elbow. His eyes were gritty, too, and they were red and burning. He coughed again. Then flashes of red flame shot before his eyes and he was suddenly awake. The cabin was on fire.

Stumbling out of his cot, he shoved open the shuttered window and began throwing out his few possessions. Cans of food, a slab of bacon and a frying pan, a couple of blankets, his coffeepot. Then he pulled the Remington and his gunbelt from their pegs by the door and stumbled out into the cool night air, trying to cough his lungs clear.

'Hardly took any time, Nix,' Meagan said. Looking up through bleary eyes Bedders could see Meagan lit by firelight holding a gun on him.

On his knees, cradling his gunbelt, Bedders asked, 'Abel, why?'

'I'm wondering if leaving the bark on them logs mighta helped keep the fire down,' Meagan said, watching the flames. Already the roof was fully engulfed and the walls were starting to catch fire. There was a loud crack and the roof shifted. Soon it would collapse completely. Meagan's hired gun, Christopher, stepped from around the far side of the cabin, a glowing torch in his hand.

'Probably saved your life, Nix, setting this blaze now. Least ways you know what a danger the cabin was. Don't pull that gun, Nix. You can't outdraw a man who's already got his gun out.'

Bedders let the hammer of his Colt down then got to his feet. Slowly, he wrapped the gunbelt around him and buckled it. A movement caught his eye and he noticed two horses at the edge of the firelight. The white mare was saddled; the other was the grey horse Baxter had ridden, the one Bedders had left in the hidden valley. Meagan looked over to the horses then back to Bedders. A corner of his mouth went up, but just a little.

'You've been holding out on me, friend,' Meagan said. 'I don't mind you getting rid of Baxter. Surprised me some, but didn't really mind it. But you keeping that valley to yourself, well, that wasn't right.'

'What's this about, then?'

'Well, Nix, I just can't trust you, is all. You hold out on me, try to steal my girl, and you go snooping around places you oughtn't. So I guess it's time we part ways.'

Bedders squared his shoulders, his gun hand twitching slightly, surprising him that he wanted to draw and fire the pistol.

'This is my valley, too.'

'No, Nix. Not any more. You've been evicted. I've packed you a couple of horses. You just ride out of here and don't look back, 'cause I'll shoot you dead.'

'Abel,' he said, trying to soften his voice, 'we're friends. We came here together.'

'You called that tune, Nix. We ain't friends any more.

You said it, not me. This is your doing.' The red of the flames roaring behind Bedders coloured Meagan's face and gave his eyes a wild look. 'So just get on that horse and ride out of here. Tell Emily goodbye, then just keep going like you always do. Once you're gone, well, she'll see how foolish it was to get ideas about you.'

'This ain't over, Abel.'

Meagan cocked his gun. 'It is, or you die right here.'

Christopher had abandoned his torch in favour of a pistol. He looked ready to shoot, too. With a great heave of his shoulders, Bedders went to the horses. He paused before getting on the white mare, remembering something. He pulled a small item from his pants pocket and tossed it to Meagan.

'What's this?' Meagan asked, catching the thing. He could see now it was a folding knife with a plain walnut handle.

'That's yours, isn't it?' Bedders said. 'That's the one you chipped opening a can of peaches on the trail up from Texas.'

Meagan opened the knife and felt along the chipped blade. Slowly, his eyes rose to meet Bedders. There was a cold fury in his voice. 'Get out of here.'

Mounting the white mare, Bedders caught up the reins of the grey horse and yanked as he started the animals off at a trot. His back tingled as he rode down the shallow hill on to the valley floor. He waited for a bullet, but it never came. Away from the firelight, he was swallowed by the early morning darkness. There was no moon and the sky only now was beginning to lighten behind him. Ahead lay the pass to Lander.

He wanted desperately to see Emily, but he would not say goodbye. Except for her, there was no reason to go to town. He would find no help there. Instead, he would have to settle this himself. Reining the mare, he turned away from the pass and urged the horses into a gallop toward the waiting valley mouth.

Emily found Meagan outside on the walk when she opened up the office for the day.

'Abel,' she said, 'you're in town early this morning.' She stood aside, letting him enter. Sweeping his hat into his hands he went to the counter, nervous energy powering him, a broad grin on his face. She found it infectious, and curious.

'I've a lot do, Emily. I believe things are looking up for me. I'm very excited about the future. I plan to come into town next week and will want to talk to you then.' He had a hard time keeping his hands folded and in front of him. He wanted to reach out and take her in his arms. 'But first things first. I want to amend my homesteading claim to include the entire valley.'

Her face fell with confusion. 'All of it?'

'Yes, of course. That's part of the big doings for me, Emily. It's going to turn things around. I know folks have soured on me some, but they'll see. I'll be a fine neighbour now that I've got my start.'

'What about Mr Bedders?'

'Of course he told you,' Meagan insisted. 'He came to town earlier today. Surely you saw him.'

'He hasn't been here, or to my house,' she said, a strain of worry tugging at her voice.

'Well, he was coming. He's up and left it all to me, Emily. The entire valley.'

'I don't believe he left.' She stiffened defiantly, her lower lip starting to quiver.

148

'What did you expect? Hell, Nix ain't never stayed around nowheres for very long.'

Fists balled, she stepped close to Meagan, a dark fury colouring her face. 'What did you do to him?'

'Nothing. Emily, really, you've got the wrong idea. I wouldn't hurt him. He's just not made for this kind of work.'

'You're a liar. And you're wrong about Morton.'

Meagan took her in his arms, pulling her close. She slapped his face, pushing away, backing through the small swinging gate beside the counter.

A dull light came into Meagan's eyes. 'He wouldn't leave without seeing you,' he said woodenly. 'No. He wouldn't go without that.'

His face twisting with hate, Meagan jammed his hat back on to his head and he strode from the office. Fighting back panic and tears, Emily heard Meagan's horse launch into a gallop and ride away.

Bedders had cleared the low hills and was making his way across the flat, empty plain that spanned the distance to the Rattlesnake Hills. The area was desolate, sparsely studded with only stubby clumps of grass and weatherworn boulders. A movement high above distracted him and he looked up to see a hawk wheeling in the clear blue sky.

Often he would look behind him, anticipating pursuit by Christopher or Meagan, or both. When he finally did spot a lone rider his stomach clenched in fear. For a moment he considered running, racing the other rider to the hills to get under cover. But he was tired of running and hiding and not doing what needed to be done.

He turned to face the oncoming rider, loosening the pistol in his holster and bringing the Remington up to rest across his saddle. After a time, as the rider's features became plainer, he relaxed.

Lincoln skidded to a stop, his horse kicking up a shower of pebbles and dragging behind it a cloud of dust. 'What are you doing out here?' he asked, a tinge of suspicion in his voice.

'Trailing a lead to your cattle.'

'I followed that fella from last night, the one who took those shots at you. Lost him a ways back but he could have come through here.'

Bedders shook his head. 'Never mind about that. I know who that was. I'll deal with him soon enough.'

Bedders explained what Meagan had done earlier that morning – about Meagan burning his house down, the threats made and Meagan's plans, and about Baxter and the hidden valley. He told Lincoln, too, about his suspicions about where Meagan was keeping the stolen cattle.

'Nobody'd keep cows out here. Ain't enough grass,' Lincoln chided.

'They're out here, all right. Somewhere in the Rattlesnake Hills. He'll take them out of there now that he has control of the entire valley.'

Lincoln shook his head. 'I can't see it. There may be room enough to hide a small herd up in those hills, but Meagan would have to come right past Cavanaugh land. I don't think he's got the nerve for that.'

'Just before he kicked me out he said I'd been snooping around and he couldn't trust me any more. That wasn't just idle talk. He knew I had been looking for his hideout. And the Rattlesnake Hills is the only place I've gone looking.'

Lincoln shifted in his saddle and cast a long look at the hills. 'You'll need some help up there.'

Smiling, Bedders said, 'I appreciate that. But we do it my way. Lefferts is up there and he's just a hired hand. Maybe he's greedy and maybe he's shady, too. But I don't want him killed. We'll get him to leave then run the herd back to Cavanaugh land.'

'What about Meagan and Christopher?'

'I can't say for Christopher. I'd like to see this finished without killing, but I don't think he'll stand for that. It's up to him. But when it's done Meagan gets two hundred head and a free pass out of the territory.'

'You're crazy!'

'My way, Lincoln. I'm sure Cavanaugh will back me, even Danelles. Do this my way or ride.'

Very slowly Lincoln said, 'And if I don't agree?'

'Then you and I are due for a dust up.'

Something cracked on Lincoln's craggy face, almost like a smile. He straightened in his saddle, letting his full height and breadth be seen. He had taken Meagan down with one punch when they first arrived. Looking at the man, Bedders thought he might last through two, if he was lucky.

'You heard me, Lincoln. Now what'll it be?'

'OK, tough guy. I'll follow you.'

Trying to hide a sigh of relief, Bedders spun his horse back toward the hills and kicked it into a gallop. Lincoln matched stride for stride and the two quickly gained on the range.

At the base of the hills, Bedders led the way around to the south, following the path he had taken the day before. He ignored the first mile or so, keeping his eyes on the broken hillcrest and along the base for hidden passes. Along the way, Lincoln told him about Devil's Gate, a gap in the hill range through which Poison Creek cut on its way down to the Sweetwater River.

They came to it by mid-afternoon. Green grass grew on either side of the deep running creek, and there were a dozen or so stunted trees along its banks. The opening into the hills was wide enough to run a herd through and deep enough to hold them, but the cattle were not there. Bedders stepped down and let his horses drink at the stream alongside Lincoln's mount. The two men walked up into the mouth of the opening, studying the ground. Although rocky in patches, and dry as a bone away from the creek, they could tell that no cattle had passed this way.

'Ever been up inside?' Bedders asked. Lincoln hadn't.

After a time they retrieved their horses and rode them into the gap.

Once inside the hills, the creek split and climbed up a shallow mound to a pool, above which was a thin waterfall that trickled down a steep, rounded rock. Further on the ground began to rise and the main creek branch disappeared into the broken face of a limestone bluff. They were in a bowl with dozens of possible paths to follow.

'Ever hear of another way in here?' Bedders asked. Lincoln shrugged.

Leaving the horses to crop grass, the two men began to search on foot for any sign of cattle or horses. After two hours, Lincoln started back for his horse.

'They're not here, Bedders. We'll head back to find Cavanaugh and talk to him about this mess,' he said.

'I'm not wrong, Lincoln.' Bedders had turned away from the big ranch foreman to look at the skyline.

'We'd've seen 'em by now, kid. I know you want to end this, and you will. Just not today.'

'There were no tracks by the creek, Lincoln. Why do you think that was?'

'Because there ain't no cattle.'

'Or they have other water.' He looked at Lincoln, who had climbed down to a level stretch and now paused. 'I'm going to follow the creeks to their source.'

Without waiting, Bedders crossed on a flat rock then dipped into a rincon at the base of a steep bluff above the creek. Buried deep in the cracked rock he saw that Poison Creek ambled this way. In the shadows of the rincon he found another pool and another thin waterfall. Working around the rock face, Bedders spotted a small game trail, barely wide enough for him to pass, worn into the hill. He saw the tracks of a jackrabbit and a coyote, but nothing larger. He waved for Lincoln to follow. The big man squeezed himself up the trail, scraping against dry rock.

They topped the hill at a slim ledge then stepped down on to a wide slab of rock. The creek cut through the slab to an elevated pond off to the right. Short, rocky spires stood like sentinels at the far edge of the stone slab. Bedders and Lincoln could hear the cows now, even before they peered around the spires. Beyond was a sloping plain filled shoulder to shoulder with cattle.

Bedders' heart sank. He knew he would find the herd but in some small corner of his mind he hoped to be wrong with his suspicions. Meagan had been even more daring and greedier than Bedders had ever imagined. He had stock from every ranch around, maybe a thousand of them, and all of them thinning for lack of grass and water.

A wild gunshot cracked and shattered some rock close to Bedders' head. He threw himself down behind the nearest spire and with a glance saw Lincoln fold his large frame behind rock, too. Crawling to his left, Bedders found a fortified corner and peeked above the rock. Lefferts was on his horse, standing in the saddle, with a rifle to his shoulder. He looked around anxiously for his targets.

'Don't be a fool, Lefferts,' Bedders called. 'We start swapping shots those cows'll panic and stampede. As tight as they're packed, you won't stand a chance.'

'I'll get you afore that, Bedders.'

'You want to be crushed by ten thousand pounds of beef? I took you for a smarter man than that. All we have to do is start shooting. We don't even have to stand up to do that.'

As if to make the point, Lincoln fired a shot into the air. Already jittery, some of the herd tried to run in the tight space. They began shoving each other and mewling in fear. Lefferts' horse was knocked about for a few seconds before he got it under control and led it away from the frightened animals. It was enough, though, to convince him; he saw what might happen if shots were fired.

'What's your play?' Lefferts asked.

'No play. You leave.'

'I gotta get something for all this, Bedders. I put in almost two years.'

'That's your loss. You've got your horse and your life. Ride on out of here with both of them and don't look back.'

'I could take a few head with me,' Lefferts suggested, his voice tight and angry. 'No one would know.'

Bedders stood from behind the rock, his rifle aimed squarely at the man.

'I'd know.' Lefferts stayed defiant for only a moment more then sank in his saddle. 'Now go. Ride out of this country, far.'

Lefferts put up his rifle and nudged his horse around until it faced down the slope. Lincoln stood up and grinned.

'Nice work, kid,' he said.

'Let's get them beeves to Cavanaugh's before Meagan shows up. There's got to be another way into this range. We'll follow Lefferts out.'

'He might be waiting. Try to ambush us.'

Bedders was about to reply when another shot snapped in the calm air, jolting the two men. Bedders happened to be looking after Lefferts and saw the man rise up in his saddle, a red hole blossoming in his back. Lefferts started to turn, trying to reach one hand spasmodically behind him, then tumbled forward off the horse.

A second shot splashed rock at Bedders, followed quickly by a third that buzzed by his ear. Lincoln snapped off a couple of quick shots, but he didn't know exactly where the shooter was hiding.

'Told Meagan to kill you!' Christopher called. 'Said he shoulda done it long ago!'

Lincoln fired two more shots sending Christopher scampering behind a rock.

'Christopher,' Lincoln yelled. 'Mr Cavanaugh told you to get out'n this country. It don't do to go against the man.'

'You started this dance, Lincoln, getting me to rile Bedders. You started this.'

While the two talked, Bedders climbed out of his fortification and worked his way back among the rocks at the edge of the bluff. He crawled slowly, trying to follow the sound of Christopher's voice. There was a cluster of boulders to his left, an island surrounded by hard-packed dirt and clumps of grass. If he could circle around and get behind the cluster he'd have a clear shot at Christopher. As he made his way, Lincoln talked and fired shots. Then all went silent except for the nervous mewling and shuffling of the cattle.

'You sneaking up on me, Lincoln?' Christopher laughed. 'Come on, then.'

The voice came from Bedders' right now, just slightly. He had no idea what Lincoln was doing but knew he had to make his move. Standing, he saw Christopher smiling at him, gun drawn.

'I wish it had been Lincoln,' he said, 'I really do.'

They both fired at the same instant, each missing. Bedders rolled to his left, up and over a boulder. The Remington came loose in his hands as a bullet skittered off the rock inches from his head. Bedders landed on all fours, pistol still in hand and fired. Christopher was behind a boulder now, only his shoulder visible. The shot went wide.

Lincoln's muffled voice said, 'Drop it!'

Christopher turned, swinging his gun around. A rifle butt caught him in the chin and sent him staggering back into the clearing, his mouth bloody.

'It's over, Christopher,' Bedders said, stepping out from cover.

Spinning wildly, swinging his gun around, Christopher turned to face Bedders. 'Damn you!' he spat. Bedders triggered once and the man collapsed, dead.

Lincoln waved his rifle, then stepped out from behind the boulder.

'I would have liked to have killed that man myself,' he said. 'Look out!'

Bedders turned and fired just as another gun sounded. He felt a tug at his injured arm and fell to the ground, the inside of his head humming. Meagan tumbled off a rock, his gun skittering off into the dust. A line of blood strafed across his temple.

Meagan got to his feet first and swept his gaze around

for the gun. Bedders staggered forward and slammed a heavy fist into Meagan's bloody temple.

'Leave him for me!' he warned Lincoln.

Meagan scooped up some dirt and threw it at Bedders' face, but Bedders knew the trick and ducked, then swept his fist back across the other's mouth. Meagan stumbled. Breathing heavily, he spat.

'You've ruined it all,' he said.

'No. I'm finally making things right.' Bedders gulped air, too. 'Get on your horse and ride. You can take two hundred head with you. No one will stop you. Just get out of the territory.'

Meagan began laughing. The sound of it rose out of him slowly until it echoed across the range.

'I ain't done,' he said.

'I've known you a long time, Abel. Is this really the fight you wanted? Do you think you're smart enough – strong enough – to take on everyone.'

'I can handle you.'

Shaking his head, Bedders said, 'And then what? Do you think you can take Lincoln here? Or Cavanaugh and the rest? How many more do you want to kill? You going to back shoot them all like Lefferts?'

Meagan answered by throwing himself at Bedders. He swung a left into Bedders' head, then a jabbing right at the man's wounded arm. Bedders cried out and spun away then brought a knee up into Meagan's stomach as the man charged again. Meagan crumpled, dropping to all fours, gasping for air. Bedders punched him in the face, then grabbed Meagan's shirt to steady him.

Bleeding from the mouth and the corner of his swelling eye, Meagan spat and said, 'I hate you. I always have.' One final punch drove Meagan to the dust.

'You leave with those cows, or I'll give you to Cavanaugh, and to hell with you.'

Bedders walked away. His shoulder hurt now from two gunshot wounds and he felt the swelling beginning to grow on the side of his face. Lincoln was leaning against a rock, grinning. Suddenly he straightened, pointed his pistol, and fired. The move was so shocking Bedders had no time to react.

Lincoln walked over to Bedders and nodded down at the ground. Meagan was dead, a small calibre revolver smoking in his lifeless hand and a black hole in his chest.

They found another way out of the Rattlesnake Hills and drove the herd to Bedders' valley. With the promise of new grass and plenty of water, the animals spread themselves out contentedly across the whole range. Lincoln said he would ride out and get Cavanaugh and round up the other ranchers, too. Bedders didn't care. He was numb. They could take it all if they wanted. Lincoln put a hand on Bedders' shoulder, saying nothing, and leaving it there for only a moment. He knew Bedders had learned a hard lesson.

'I wouldn't have killed him if he had taken your deal,' Lincoln said.

Bedders nodded. Meagan had given neither of them a choice. He thought of the graves they had dug for the three dead men, thought of the loneliness up on that scraggily range. His friend had deserved better. But Meagan had stopped being his friend a long time ago. At the end he was nothing more than a back-shooting rustler.

As Lincoln was about to leave they spotted movement at the bend in the valley, at Bedders' burned-out house. Leaving the cattle, the two rode in to investigate. Cavanaugh was there sifting through the ashes. Emily was with him.

She ran to him as he got down from the white mare and threw her arms around his neck. Lincoln grimaced a little then shrugged and went over to Cavanaugh.

'I thought he'd killed you,' she cried, tears streaming down her face.

'No,' he said, then kissed her. After a moment he looked up at Cavanaugh who was walking over to him.

'Lincoln just told me what happened, son. That was tough.'

'It's over now. If you want me gone, too, I'll take what's mine and leave.' Emily's fingers bit deeply into his arm.

'I think we're done with this business all together. Time to get you back on your feet.' Cavanaugh turned and pointed at the stone and ash mess that had been Bedders' home. 'Tomorrow we'll have a passel of men out here to rebuild this house. And maybe we can get you a barn raised, too.'

'And I'll have the women out here,' Emily said, excitedly, 'with enough food to feed them.'

'I was thinking, Mr Cavanaugh, that we should build the house a mite bigger this time. Something large enough for a family.'

Bedders looked down at Emily, smiling and nodding her approval, and squeezed her close. Holding her he looked out on the valley, his heart seeing a milling herd of white-faced cattle scattered about and a pineboard house at the edge of the cool pond. Next to that was a corral filled with fine, fiery horses, and a hay barn bulging with golden bales. These were no longer strange images for his mind to conjure. Finally, they would become real.